i

THE YOUNG MOLLY MAGUIRES

Young Passages
in the era of the Robber Barons

J. E. O'Rourke

Library of Congress Control Number: 2015907699

ISBN-13: 978-0692411360

ISBN-10: 0692411364

GAELWRITER PUBLISHERS

An imprint of J. E. O'Rourke
P.O. Box 335
Manchester, CA 95459

Books by the same author

LEAVING MAJOR TELA, a YA novel

Acknowledgements

For the historical period, some of the outline and details of the Molly Maguire's time can be obtained from archives of the contemporary newspapers as well as in the sensationalized fiction published in magazines and periodicals of the 1870s. General working conditions of the miners can be found in reports of miners union officials, and some underground mine conditions were informed by the author's own experience as an engineer in eastern and western underground coalmines. An historical coverage of the Molly experience is given in the masterful, *Making Sense of the Molly Maguires*, by Kevin Kenny, published in 1998

A Molly Maguire Lament

God lifted noble man from earth

crowned him lord of all creation

until a stunning fall from grace

banished him to a life of toil and sweat

Impoverished men reentered earth

pillaging black coal so they might live

Our Miners toiled mightily to earn their bread

How so, earth's new Owners demanded more

Till the Miners raised up a young prophet, Union,

to lead a way from slavery,

but Union could not strike water from the rock,

and our Miners withered in despair

A new Joshua rose up to besiege the Owners,

as the Molly Maguires entered the fray

smoting Owners' captains from ramparts and wall,

Until undone by perfiidy of church and state

Who struggle for justice, sing a lament for the Mollies,

though brutal men struck from both their camps

it is forever the victor who writes our history,

and cartloads of Mollies swung in the air

PREFACE

Not a lot is known about the inner workings of the Molly Maguires, a secret society of Irish miners who worked in the anthracite coalmines of northeastern Pennsylvania during a twenty-year period ending about 1875. The Mollies left no written accounts of their organization or the actions they conducted against the railroad company owners of the mines in that era of labor unrest and violence. In newspapers and periodicals of the time, the Mollies were most often demonized as cutthroats and murderers. They were surely involved in labor violence, but the vastly unequal balance of power between mine owners and laborers made a tragic outcome all but certain.

This is a fictional story of some younger members of the Molly families, a handful of teenage boys and a girl, who themselves worked in the coal mines, and who understood their fathers were surely Molly Maguires—and the likely outcome of that.

TABLE OF CONTENTS

CHAPTER ONE—Breaker Boys

Inside the fence, a wooden breaker building stood gaunt on tall, spindly wood legs, straddling piles of dusty coal and conveyor belts. Like a giant bug, watching from its lair. The sloped breaker building was designed to lift tons of coal and rock from a mine shaft beneath its upper end, pound the material to pieces beneath a thundering row of stamping mills, and send the pieces sliding down long wooden chutes to the building's lower end. Breaker boys sat on a dozen rows of wood benches laid across the chutes, cursing, coughing, launching lead and refrain of bawdy songs, struggling to keep up with the endless task of picking out lumps of shale rock from the coal as it streamed beneath them. At the bottom of the chutes, the coal dropped into a long line of waiting railroad cars.

All that was on any working day, but today was not a working day. A breeze kicked up clouds of coal dust along the railroad tracks. The black dust swirled about the legs of the breaker, and no sounds came from the building. From outside a chain link fence, Owen and his friend, Peter, looked in at the desolate scene.

"Wouldn't it be grand if we could go back in as underground workers," Owen said. He knotted his fingers in the wire mesh fencing and shook his head. "Breaker boys—what a pair of flaming successes we've been. We're probably the oldest boys working in the breaker."

"Right, but at least we'll be at work again, isn't it?" Peter said. "Along with my da and yours. We'd all be eating grasshoppers if the strike went on much longer."

"Yes, but it isn't enough that they busted the union," Owen said, "sure, now they've got their blacklist, too. Look over to the shack there; someone's written on the poster."

They went closer to the empty guard shack. The poster tacked on the wall gave the names of men fired for breaking company work rules and organizing labor troubles. Posters like this were hung in all the mines of the surrounding hills, warning mine bosses against hiring any of the named troublemakers. A crude, red crayon picture of a pistol had been hand-drawn on the poster, followed by a scrawled message:

Notis this has been caried far enough—M.M.

"Well, the mine super may be in a bit of a shave, now," Peter said.

"Looks like the work of our Molly Maguires."

"Our Mollies—likely you shouldn't be saying that out loud," Owen said. "The railroad cops might like to talk about the killings of a few mine bosses with a lad on such friendly footing with the Mollies."

Peter glanced around. "Aye, but isn't it grand the way the Mollies got in the fight? They'll straighten things out for the workers better than the bleeding union was able to do."

"Come away from it, Peter; don't make too light of what they're after doing. They're outlaws now, and if they're taken they could be hanged." Owen turned away from the poster. "Worse, still, you can't tell where your own da might be in all of it. We'd better hope things ratchet down a few notches before it's too late for everyone."

CHAPTER TWO—Coffin Notice

Owen came down a pathway off the road. His house was like its neighbors in the Pennsylvania mine patch, a small, wood plank house, blackened by films of rain and coal dust. The house sat on a level piece of ground notched into a steep hillside. A few narrow terraces of vegetable garden stair-stepped down the slope from the backyard. In a corner of the backyard a wood-shingled, peaked roof on wooden posts covered an outdoor cooking stove and clay oven.

Finding no one in the yard, he scanned the garden terraces below. His mother wasn't there either, probably off hauling water from the community spigot. He went back into the house; the main room was empty and the door to his parent's bedroom was closed. Now might be a good time to take a closer look at the paper he'd found. He went to his own room, a lean-to addition built onto the house at a time when his older brothers were still in the house. The room had just enough space for a double-deck bunk, a steamer trunk at the foot, and a small desk and chair. A diffused daylight filled the room from a narrow horizontal window, high above the desk.

Owen opened the desk drawer and took out a paper retrieved from the wood stove that morning. He unfolded it and carefully smoothed the crumpled and scorched surface. A crude drawing of a revolver and a coffin were at the top of the sheet, with hand printed text below:

> *yer blaklisd better cum down by nite and men hire bak or this will be eur haus.*

It was signed with initials, *M.M.* The last two words of the message had been crossed out, re-written, and crossed out again. Owen froze as the front door opened and closed. He shoved the note back into the drawer, listened to the footsteps and a chair being dragged across the floor. He waited a few seconds and stepped out of his room.

His father, Liam Dougherty, sat looking out the window. Straight, gray black hair, drooping black mustache, big hands clasped on the tabletop. Both he and Owen's mom had come over from Ireland as children with their families, and Liam started working in the breaker when he was only ten years-old. When he'd married and had sons, he'd insisted that they would finish grade school, though most boys in the mine patch had just a few years of schooling before going into the mines. He couldn't really fathom what doors an education might open, but it seemed important, and it was something he wanted for his sons.

"Da, I just got in myself. Peter and I were up at the mine to see what all was happening. The engineer had some steam up for the pumps and was testing the hoist wheels. I guess everything is set for us to go back in Monday?"

"Aye, well, it's over for now. Five months of striking, near-starving our families, and for what? The organizers had some grand notions of what a union could do for us, and where's it all gone to? The blessed union is demolished. The railroad will make up any of their losses by cutting wages again, but some workers might have to see a child or two die before they iron out their own debts."

Owen felt the despair and anger in his father's words. "The Molly Maguires left a message on Mr. Jones' blacklist. It said things had been carried far enough, and they showed a drawing on it of a pistol and coffin. What do you think is going to happen now?"

"The mine superintendent, Mr. Jones, was assassinated last night," Liam said.

CHAPTER THREE— Loyalties & Secrets

MINE SUPERINTENDANT SLAIN—special to Mountain Herald, April 26, 1875:

"Mr. James Jones was shot and killed last night on his way home from a late meeting at the offices of the Reading Railroad. There were no witnesses, but judging by threats he had received it is once again the work of the Molly Maguires. This and other recent killings show the depravity and cutthroat nature of Irish miners who dominate our region. They inflict their murderous rage on any who oppose them. Not since the Assassins of Persia or the Thugs of India have there been such a bloodthirsty lot as the men who call themselves Molly Maguires. Indeed, if things do not soon change, it will be the right of our Pennsylvania citizens to use the example of San Francisco in dealing with their own lawlessness during the gold rush of 1849. Today it may be time to mete out that same vigilante justice here."

Owen stared at the newspaper for a long time after he'd picked it up from the table and read the piece. He didn't know anything about the Assassins of Persia or the Thugs of India, but the Irish miners and those other people were all of a kind in this sort of bad cess.

"Da, do you think the Mollies, if they did it, were they right?"

"Was Jones right to take away the livelihood of the eleven men on the blacklist, and only for supporting our union? For a miner, a fair and decent wage is needed for his family to live. How can they be denied this? Lesser tyrannies, like the English King's taxes, had been enough for Americans to take up the gun."

Owen leaned back into his chair and stared across the table, alarmed, absently watching out the window at his mother moving about the stove outside. Da was always the one for the American Revolution. People didn't care about the wages of immigrant Irish miners, though. "A few shops in town have signs in their windows saying Irish immigrants will never become true Americans, and they should be kicked out," Owen said.

Liam's jaw muscles tensed and his clenched hands trembled until he had his anger damped. "I've seen the signs. A couple of the same shop owners bought a son's way out of the draft rather than let them fight in our country's Civil War. True Americans, is it? Our family gave all we had, both your brothers, sent off to enlist with the

Irish Brigade and with my own blessings." He looked down at his clasped hands, tightening them till the knuckles shone white. "Next month it will be twelve years since they fell fighting the Rebs at Chancellorsville."

Owen glanced past his da's shoulder at the wall calendar. Yes, almost May, already. It figured; each year his mother felt her worst about now. He'd heard from his da how she'd objected to sending both boys. Sean was only seventeen when he died, and she hadn't ever forgiven da for letting Sean go.

His mom, Aine, came in carrying two steaming mugs of wild herb tea, and set them on the table with spoons. She took pieces of honeycomb from her apron and laid a few bits near each cup, and, abruptly as she'd entered, went back outside.

Owen gathered up his fragments of honeycomb and stirred them into his tea, trying to think how to say it. "I wondered, Da, whether you could tell me if you're one of the Molly Maguires?"

A startled look came into Liam's eyes and he passed a cupped hand over his moustache and jaw. "A bold question, son, but we'd better put that sort of talk to rest."

CHAPTER FOUR—Kevin's Shanty

That night after a striker's subsistence supper of tea and wheat crackers, Owen started up to Kevin Boyle's shanty on the upper slope of the mountain. It had been a year since Owen began visiting the shanty as a way of meeting and talking with the old miner's niece, Maura. She visited her uncle almost every evening to see that he ate at least one cooked meal for the day. She and Owen had been close friends since their last years of grammar school, and Owen felt at an awkward place. He figured he was expected to act a bit older now, but wasn't entirely sure what all that included.

During the long strike, he had brought a few of his friends up to meet Kevin. He'd welcomed such visits and the boys gathered at their new clubhouse a couple of times a week now. Kevin's tales of his life and work as a miner in Ireland, England and America, were endlessly fascinating to the boys. Owen often came up alone to join Kevin on walks to the old abandoned mines in the surrounding mountains, and to hear from him about the skills needed in the miner's craft.

As Owen climbed the hillside the sun edged behind the distant ridges and a chill seeped into the air. Still, wasn't it grand? The great sweep of it, away from all that black coal dust covering the houses and stunting the trees below. But even up here, he knew Kevin had not escaped the black dust entirely; it was heavy in his lungs now, and had forced him to retire. Kevin's shanty lay ahead, wedged into a rocky hillside. A thick, low hedge of thorny briar came off the slope and wrapped around a flat, half-circle yard out in front. A tall wooden arch with a swinging gate interrupted the hedge.

Kevin came to the door after Owen knocked and waved him inside.

Peter turned and looked him up and down, "Owen, have you no scones with you for our tea?"

He was the same age as Owen, sixteen. Patrick Cahill, fourteen, sat next to Peter; Tim Donnelly, thirteen, the other side of the potbelly stove; and Thomas Roarty, fifteen, beside Tim.

"Ah, no, but I've an appetite for the tea," Owen said.

"No scones—what a chiseler," Peter said. "A good thing we're saving the real tea for holy days. Maura made this; she snipped

14

some of Kevin's old leather shoelaces. Not bad, though, gives it a smoky taste."

Maura came in the back door as he spoke and set a kettle on the stove. "Don't believe a word he says, Owen. It's not the real stuff anymore, of course, mostly plantain and slippery elm bark now." She poured Owen a cup of tea and drew up a wood crate to sit among the boys.

Owen slipped off his sweater and pulled up a stool. Kevin went to sit on a cushioned, peeled willow couch set back against the wall. He shook with a coughing spell. The boys' talk resumed, all about the Jones' shooting.

"A couple of mine workers from over at the Shamokin side were in my da's saloon before the shooting," Thomas said. "And two men on the blacklist came in to talk with them."

Chairs creaked in the quiet and a fire snapped in the iron stove. "Maybe those Shamokin men were the Mollies who did the mine superintendent," Peter said.

"It's the way of the Mollies, isn't it?" Thomas said. "Move some strangers in for the job, so it's harder to fix them."

The boys lapsed into quiet, until Owen turned to Kevin, "How'd the

Mollies get that name?"

Kevin leaned forward, arms propped across his knees. "It was the name of a secret society in Ireland, small tenant farmers being evicted so the landlords could use the land for the better-paying sheep. The Mollies dressed like banshees, wearing long dresses and going through the fields at night slaughtering the sheep. It got worse, and a couple of landlord agents were killed. After that a swath of Mollies were rounded up and hanged. That finished the raids, and the farmers, too. Boatloads of families immigrated to here, and no doubt some sworn Mollies with them. They were violent men who took the wrong turn then, and it's happening again now."

Kevin took a fit of coughing, ending his story. An eight-hooter, barred owl called mournfully from outside.

"I wish I was older so they'd ask me to join," Peter said.

The room went quiet. The air vent knob in the stove door warbled and the hot metal stovepipe made clicking noises. All the boys looked to Owen and waited.

"The Mollies have killed some mine bosses. What about that?" Owen said.

Peter fidgeted in his chair. "Yes, but what about the railroad don't care how many miners they kill every year getting the coal out on the cheap, right?"

"There's maybe a bit of a difference here, isn't it?"

"You're saying we don't owe the Mollies a thing for what they're trying to do for the mineworker?"

"I don't know. Are the Mollies right in the sort of fighting they're doing? Or is Father Morrison right, and it's only going to get them condemned to Hell?"

Peter looked annoyed, as he sometimes did when his best friend wouldn't accept his point. But Owen feared that Father Morrison might be right, and where did that put his da?

CHAPTER FIVE—Confraternity

Sunday morning Owen tumbled out of bed at the first light of dawn sliding through the window. He dressed and hurried to split firewood so his mother could start the stove. She was already chopping away at a log before he made it out of the house, and he took the axe from her. While she prepared breakfast Owen split wood till he was lightheaded and weak, the effects of increasingly sparse meals in the recent months. He stopped chopping to carry wood to the bin. His mother had mixed a lump of soda bread dough, no more than a fistful, and added wild buckwheat she'd collected on the hillsides. She put the bread in the oven and knelt at the firebox while he handed her pieces of kindling. When the fire was going, they sat on stools and watched flames flicker from the low opening.

"Finally, after all this terrible long time, we'll be going back in tomorrow," Owen said. His mother remained silent. "Five whole months and we didn't gain a thing—nothing for it now but to take a pay cut."

Aine sat up straight, hands clasped in her lap, and watched the fire. She was forty-eight years old, black hair swept back and clasped, not many lines in her face, just near the eyes and mouth, pale skin, thin and tall.

"I don't suppose you'd like to go for a walk while the oven's heating," Owen said. "The swallows are back, building nests along the cliffs." He waited, but she made no sign she'd even heard. She probably saw the birds anyhow, along the pathway up to her refuge. He'd followed her up there a few times without her ever knowing, high up onto a ridge top, where she'd sit near an edge and look out over the hills. She hadn't ever gone to church for as long as he could remember, only up to her refuge on Sundays, while Owen and his da were at Mass.

They sat at the stove a while, till she got up and used a long-handled ash peel to slide the loaf into the oven. She took up a bucket then and started off for the public water spigot. Owen grabbed the bucket handle, but she shook her head, smiled, and eased his hand away. He watched her walk off, ignoring another woman who called to her on her way to get water, too. The sun was just lifting above the hazy lines of mountaintops as Owen turned to go back into the house and get ready for Mass.

Inside the church Father Morrison paced in front of the altar rail. He recounted the litany of assassinations during the past months, and now, Superintendent Jones. He looked out at the rows of men, women, and children and swatted his sermon notes against an open palm. "We see each day more and more of the evils some men have brought into our community. 'For some men love darkness more than the light.' Why do we tolerate such devils in our midst? They have bound themselves by their insidious secret oaths against the rule of law under the government, and against the teachings of Holy Mother Church. Violence, terror, murder, these are the signs you shall know them by. The Church has condemned them and their deeds in the past, in Ireland, and so, too, it condemns them today, here and now. Some of these men may be sitting among you. Think not what they do is out of regard for justice—it is from a murderous, false pride, spawned of Satan, himself..."

Owen glanced beside him at his father. Liam's face was set as unreadable as slate and his arms were folded across his chest. Owen took a deep breath. Condemned must be the same as a mortal sin. Da never went to confession, but surely he would ask God for forgiveness, supposing there wasn't any time left for confession. But what kind of thinking was that? He shuddered and tried to clear his mind. Would this sermon never be over?

Sunday night was confraternity class, and Owen headed over to the parish hall. The hall was a long, wood frame building set square to the back of the church. When he entered Fr. Morrison was speaking from a lectern on the stage at one end of the hall. There were already about thirty girls and as many boys seated in chairs out front. Owen took a seat in the last row, beside Peter, as Fr. Morrison continued talking. He was into the Bible story about the laborers.

Owen slumped in his chair and pictured the scene as he listened. The owner rounds up these idle laborers early in the morning to work in his vineyards, offering them a denarius, some sort of coin, for the day, and they're glad to get the work. Around mid-morning the owner goes out and finds more men, also idle, offers the same wages, and they go with him to the vineyard. The owner goes out again late in the day and wouldn't you know it—more idle men. He hires them, too, and they go to work alongside the others in the blazing heat. Along comes evening and it's time for the owner to pay his workers. He gives the last ones hired each a denarius for the day's work. Then, when he finally comes to the first-hired, they each get just a denarius, too. They grumble about the unfairness and the owner tells them to take their money and get going. Wasn't that the wages agreed on? Were they envious because he chose to be generous to some? And the gospel writer, Matthew, sums it up: the last will be first and the first shall be last.

Fr. Morrison paused to let it all sink in a bit. Owen squirmed in his chair. There was something mean and narrow about the parable. If the owner had enough money that he could afford to be so generous with the last, he might have paid at least a little more to the first. But no, he had to show who held the power, and workers had to accept whatever generosity they might get from the owner— and no disrespectful grumbling, either.

"All right lads, what's the message here? Who'll start us off?" Fr. Morrison said.

Owen glanced at Peter. Probably Peter didn't like that parable either, screwing up his mouth and wrinkling his brow. Owen nudged him and whispered, "Wouldn't have been any problem at all if the laborers had a good union. They'd have had steady work at honest wages for everyone." Peter looked at him and Owen nodded toward the stage. Peter grinned, jumped to his feet, and blurted out what Owen had said.

"You dunce—sit down!" Fr. Morrison shouted at him. Peter dropped like a breaker weight and Owen ducked low behind the guy in front to keep out of Father's sight. "Union, indeed," Fr. Morrison said. "Labor combinations are no more than an attempt to extort money from the owner of an enterprise. The owner, according to his own conscience, may make a just offer, and it is up to the individual workman to accept it or not. Or are we all instead to become Communists, Mr. Reilly?"

Peter glanced red-faced at Owen, who smiled back. "No, Father," Peter answered, rising again. "Slip of the tongue, sorry."

"Good—remain standing and give us the meaning of the parable's message of the last shall be first and the first, last." Peter groaned and shook a hidden fist at Owen.

After the discussions the youths cleared the floor and stacked chairs along one wall. An old, retired miner mounted the stage with a fiddle, and was followed by a girl with a flute. For most of the youths, this was the best part of confraternity. Owen wasn't too good with the dancing, but he was mad to feel the music. Most of his bunch, except young Tim, got into the lineup for the first reel, *The Siege of Carrick*. A line of boys faced off with a line of girls and there was lots of jostling as boys shoved and pushed to get opposite someone they liked. Maura wound up at one end of the girl's line with no boy opposite her. She was a lanky, thin girl from having had Rickets when she was young, but she was wiry and tough, too. Owen smiled; he liked the wild look of her. She had a head on her rising toward the back like a breaker and hair glinting black as coal hanging almost to her belt. He walked out and stood across from her.

"Want to blunder through this thing together?" he said.

"Speak for yourself Owen Dougherty—blunder!" she said. "I know how to dance well enough."

Owen grinned, and with that the music started and the two lines closed. Maura and Owen went flying around each other, first the one way, then another, crossed with the next couple to do the same, and back into line before they got run over by a couple coming down the middle. It was complete mad fun and confusion as they gradually made their way up to the head of the line.

After finishing that piece and *The Wind That Shakes the Barley*, the musicians packed it in. Some of the older boys and girls stayed together to talk, while the younger ones tore off in all directions. Maura and Owen hung close, but before they had a chance to say much Fr. Morrison beckoned. He was sitting on the edge of the stage and Owen went over to him.

"You hardly participate in any of our discussions, Owen, unless it's to embolden one of your cohorts to make some rash remark. The ironical wit of Mr. Reilly's comment was out of character for him, but perhaps not for his seating mate. You're as bright and quick-witted as your brother, Sean, when he was your age, but less inclined to the faith."

Owen felt a small sting of regret that he was disappointing Fr. Morrison. He'd heard from his da how the priest had had fond hopes that Sean might go into a seminary to study for the priesthood, and how stunned he'd been when Sean abruptly left with his older brother to fight in the war.

"Yes, Father, I know, our Sean had a powerful faith, but I'll stay firm in my own faith and work as a miner."

"A miner. An honest vocation, to be sure, but not, perhaps, the highest calling God had in mind for you. Your father, hard as the man seems, had the grace to allow you to finish grammar school— an advantage few others of these boys have had. Why take such light down into the dark pocket of a breasting chamber where it can inspire so few? Think hard on it, Owen. Remember what I told you.

The diocese could provide you with a scholarship to a good boarding school in Philadelphia, and from there it's on to the seminary."

Owen nodded; Fr. Morrison made it very hard to stay clear without seeming disrespectful. "I've thought about it, Father, but it's a miner I want to be," Owen said.

CHAPTER SIX—Back to Work

Monday morning was dark, cold, and damp when the boys climbed the stairs to the breaker. There wasn't much joking and shoving among them; there'd been too many months with barely enough to eat. Still, they'd had a good winter in some ways, sledding down hills after a snowfall, hunting for rabbits with a large-bore, black powder rifle that'd knock your shoulder off. Well, maybe that sort of free time and fun was over and done with, but at least they'd be eating regular again.

The steam whistle blew and the walls and floor shook as the machinery rumbled into life. They came off the stairway and walked up a beam alongside the chutes. Deak Williams and his cohort slid into the lowest two rows, reserved by the boss for the Welsh lads, and the rest of the breaker boys, mostly Irish, split off by fives as they went farther up to their own benches.

A new Irish lad was usually placed high up in the first rows, where there was plenty of sharp edged waste rock, slate, coming down with the coal. If the boy had friends he might be given a place farther down. Older hands often moved down to newly open positions, where a little less of picking slate might be needed. Owen and Peter chose to remain in row four of the twelve rows in the breaker. They had the natural caution of some miners against tempting fate, by changing a work spot for no sound reason. There were enough cripples in town and new headstones cropping up in the graveyard every year to remind them of chance accidents waiting to happen. Maybe there wasn't too much could happen in the breaker, other than falling into the hoppers at the end of the chutes, but they weren't always going to be breaker boys.

The first couple of hours Owen's back ached. He had cramps in his legs pushing against the coal from running too fast beneath him, and he could hardly reach down to grab another piece of slate. His hands had been tough last December, but now the knife-sharp edges of the slate were nicking him again. Just not as bad as when he first started to work in the breaker.

About nine o'clock the first boy fainted and his buddies grabbed him before he fell. A half-hour later another boy keeled over and fell onto the chute, and the boys in the next row hauled him back up. The breaker boss saw what bad shape they were in, and he sent out for bread. Later, about ten o'clock, he walked along the chutes and passed out chunks of bread. He kept notes for the paymaster to take deductions from the boys' pay envelopes. That bread would not come cheap. The boys ate while they continued to pick slate, and if there was no butter on the bread there was plenty of spicy soot. It cut the hunger pangs, and they were all right until lunch break.

The boys gathered on the field behind the breaker at noon. Usually they'd all have eaten their lunch on the sly by now, so that they might kick around a ball, but no one had the energy today. Owen opened his lunchbox and found radishes, a few sprigs of a wild plant called miner's lettuce, a handful of huckleberries, and a few pieces of honeycomb. Between gardening and gathering edible wild plants, his mother did all right.

"Do you think we'll ever get promoted out of that damned breaker?" Peter said. "I've been in there almost five years now."

Owen felt the same restlessness. He'd been there only two years, but both were already past an age when breaker boys might be given a chance to work underground. Peter had been held back because he'd had some run-ins with the breaker boss and a couple of fistfights with the Welsh. Owen wondered if he was being held back because he'd had the pretensions of getting an education before taking his place in the mines. He tried hard, though, to keep up his optimism.

"They'll be drafting some of us out of the breaker when things get going again," Owen said. "I heard a few of the single men have drifted off to work at the coal mines in Colorado while we were out on strike. That'll probably open up some jobs all along the line."

"Right, so, could be a half-dozen in that, but they'll probably promote only the Welsh to move up," Peter said. "Our man Deak and his friends will be first in line, even though they only just got off the boat a couple months before our strike."

"They're going to save two spots for us, Peter, you'll see. It'll be our chance."

"Think so? Maybe. I hope so."

Thomas asked, "What about tomorrow—we going to have our bonfire for Beltaine again this year?"

"You're right, it's the Eve tomorrow. Yes, the bonfire—why not? Can't break with tradition," Owen said.

Each year bonfires were lighted on hilltops the night before May First, to mark Beltaine, signaling the end of winter darkness and the welcoming of bright summer days. Old-timers from places like

Donegal and Mayo had kept such Celtic tradition alive, though Fr. Morrison warned pagan practices associated with Beltaine and the funeral wakes were a danger to one's faith. The boys always held a bonfire anyway.

"I wonder if the Welsh bunch will try catching us out again?" Tim said.

The Welsh boys were well aware of the annual Irish celebration, and as part of the ongoing rivalry, they had searched out and ambushed them at their bonfire the previous year. Owen and his friends had gotten the worst of that.

Owen snapped shut his lunch box and stood up. "Right, we need to talk about that, but for now it's back to the breaker."

Owen stopped off at Kevin's house after work. He was exhausted, but knew if he went home first and laid down even for a minute he wouldn't wake up again till it was time to go back to work. He was glad to find Maura there, because he needed help from them both. He described his plan for the Beltaine celebration.

"Are you crazy?" Maura said. But she was half-laughing, too. Kevin shook his head but took them to his tool shed to get supplies.

CHAPTER SEVEN—Beltaine

That evening, as the last shades of light reached into the creek bottom, the boys made a final check of preparations. It was the same place they'd used for last year's bonfire. The tumbled-in stonewalls of the roofless mill, and the huge, broken skeleton of a timber-framed water wheel, gave an eerie appearance to the place. The nearly dry creek had drained into old mine workings underlying the valley, and had caused the mill to be abandoned long ago. Most of the planks that could be scavenged had been removed over the years, carted off to build workers' shanties.

They heaped a pile of dried limbs and brush in a sunken ground area beside the mill. The large, bowl-shaped depression was all that was left of a forebay that flowed to the mill's water wheel. Afterward they sat on a crumbling, low earth embankment encircling the forebay, and passed a beer bucket Thomas had snatched from his da's saloon. All about them the big trees pressed in. A horned moon rose in the heavens, and long, slow-moving clouds edged past, sending shadows sliding over the pearly white ground.

The boys took turns telling the strangest tales they knew. All of them could tell tales of the *Sidhe*, the Other-Folk, or faery people, but Thomas and Patrick were masterful at putting the horror and strangeness into a tale. Who could tell if the tales held some truth? Adults they knew swore by the truth of them. In the lives of poor people death came painfully early, oftentimes in a terrible manner. Though one did not doubt the saving grace of the church, it was not wise to question what might exist outside the light of faith. And the Welsh, another Celtic people, had their own supernatural tales, and that might help unravel them, too, if Owen had his guess.

As Thomas related one of his stories the boys kept glancing toward the gaping black window openings in the upper walls of the mill. They were all anxious. Thomas was in the middle of a particularly horrifying scene, when Peter hissed and everyone listened. Owen wagged his hand to keep Thomas talking. The snapping of twigs and the rustle of underbrush edged in between Thomas' words— and stopped whenever he paused in his story.

Owen signaled and Peter and Tim ran out to the center of the forebay. Tim splashed a tin of kerosene onto the pile and Peter tossed a match. The flames raced through the spindly brush, and the boys stood on the embankment as Tim sang, *Hag of Bones*. Within minutes the brush pile crackled and hummed with a fierce energy, and the boys rubbed smarting eyes and poked each other, watching all the while toward the woods. They hadn't long to wait; figures popped above the embankment on the far side. As the intruders spread out and circled behind the fire, Owen turned to the mill building and waved his arm.

A shrieking, witch-like figure cloaked in black and with long black hair streaming behind her flew from an upper window. Amid shouts of "The Hag—the Hag—she came to our song!" the apparition swooped toward the fire, shaking a bit like a witch with palsy, and Owen tossed his pouch. A small explosion and poof of smoke erupted from the flames, showering everyone with blazing twigs. The Welsh boys ducked and careened about as the witch sailed through the cloud of smoke, screaming horribly and flying at about eight feet off the ground.

The Welsh boys broke and ran. Peter and Thomas caught up with two laggards and swung at them with sticks as they clambered over the embankment. Owen scrambled across to where the Hag had sailed over the embankment. On the other side, Maura lay in a rocky brush pile with eyes shut and arms and legs akimbo, her cape torn and held fast in the brush. A short distance away a wood seat hung from an overhead cable and trolley block.

Owen knelt beside her, nudged her shoulder, and put his ear close to her mouth. He couldn't make out if she was breathing, and he was terrified. She must have lost her seating when the pouch of blasting powder went off, and after Kevin had warned him to go easy with the powder. The others came up behind and watched as he tore her cape loose from the brush and picked her up.

"I've got to get her to Kevin's—he'll know what to do."

Owen pushed through them and started running. Maura was light but it was awkward carrying her. He kept going, only slowing to a walk when he had to catch his breath. The boys stayed with him till Tim broke away and ran ahead to alert Kevin. Owen about fell through the opened door when he reached the shanty, and stumbled inside to lay Maura on the bench. Kevin placed a kerosene lamp on a crate nearby and sat beside her. He leaned close, lifted her eyelid, then felt about her head and throat as Owen told him what happened. Finally, he sat up and smoothed a hand over her head, combing his fingers through the hair, looking down at her. She's gone Owen thought, and he wanted to die, too.

"She'll be all right, just a knot at the back of her head," Kevin said. "Fill the basin with water from the spring and we'll coax her around."

Owen was so relieved he almost knocked Thomas over as he went out the door. He filled a steel basin at the hillside spring and hurried back into the shanty. A coughing spell forced Kevin up from the bench and he flipped a cloth to Owen and motioned him toward Maura. Owen sat and frantically sponged her forehead.

"Not so much, you'll drown her," Peter said. The water streamed off Maura, ran through the willow slats on the bench, and onto the floor. They all crowded close looking for signs. Minutes passed, and finally she stirred. Her eyes opened and she lifted a hand to touch gingerly at the back of her head. She was a sight—wide black rings around her eyes from burnt cork, and a garish job of scarlet lipstick—a terrific Hag. Her eyes flicked from one to the other of the boys, and came to rest on Owen. "You should try breathing smoke like that yourself sometime," she said, annoyed and tired sounding. "I almost dropped off the stupid cable into the fire." Owen was so choked up he could only nod.

CHAPTER EIGHT—Morris

By the end of the week the boys were almost back to working shape. It didn't take as long now to stir up from their benches when the machines stopped pounding at the end of a day. As for promotions to miners' jobs left by people who'd moved away, it didn't look like there would be any. The superintendent had brought in blacklegs, what the miners called men who'd worked at a mine that remained open during a strike. A Welshman and a Cornishman—they were the ones got the empty chambers. That pushed angry feelings even higher among former union men.

The following week the railroad's Coal and Iron Police arrested a man suspected of being a Molly and an accomplice in the Jones assassination. Jim Tully was young, single, and a mine laborer who boarded at the house of a widow in Shamokin. She had young children and took in boarders like him just to survive. Tully denied the shooting, or even being a Molly, and claimed the only group he belonged to was the Ancient Order of Hibernians, the AOH, a fraternal order of Irish mine workers. However, the police suspected the Mollies were an inner circle of the AOH, and the Church did, too, considering the AOH as shadowy as the Mollies. It distrusted any organization that held secret meetings, rituals, hand signals, and all such ceremonial trappings. Jim Tully was immediately clapped in jail.

Meanwhile Owen's father was spending a lot of time away from the house each evening, and Owen became increasingly worried. He hardly ever got to sleep at night before knowing his father had arrived safely at home. He tried several times to find out what his mother knew of the situation, but she remained as distant as in all the years of his growing up. He worried that that might never change.

Maura joined Owen during a lull in activities at the next confraternity meeting. She felt better, but wouldn't be doing any dancing—she still had a bruise on her head. Owen picked up a copy of the Mountain Herald that Fr. Morrison had left on the bench and began reading. It was as bad as the earlier one his da had brought home:

The Mollies are thought to have branches all over the region, and are likely responsible for much of the labor unrest and crime that are eating away at our nation. There is an inherent depravity of these criminals; they are bloodthirsty, obdurate, and fiendish— unfit for freedom. The military must be called in to help keep peace in the coalfields, and to shoot down any violent agitators and criminals that are caught red-handed. It is high time, too, for our citizens to consider vigilante justice.

Maura read alongside him. He waited till she leaned back in her chair and he put down the paper. "I can hardly understand his prattle, but it's not hard to get the ugly tone of it," he said.

"It's difficult to live in the coal patch. Don't you ever wish you could go live somewhere else?" Maura said.

"What would I do, work in a factory? Not me—mining is a job that puts you to the test every day. The way Kevin tells it, not even a soldier going into battle gets closer to God than a miner going down to his work chamber."

Maura bunched a corner of her mouth, swept back some loose strands of hair from her face, and reset the hair clip. "Gripping, that. I hope God cares a bit for the ordinary laborer, too, because they don't seem to be moving too many Irish up the ranks to become full miners."

"I'll make it. It might have been easier with a union, but the Mollies will break the Welsh hold, and the Mollies will help force fair wages from the owners, too."

She looked at him wide-eyed, "The Mollies—so now you're wanting to believe in them? Owen, the man in this paper wants Jim Tully hanged and every other Molly they can find. He doesn't care whether the railroad police or some vigilantes do the job, either."

"So what do we do—just swallow our courage and give up?" He shoved the paper aside. "I don't know what's to be done," he said. "Examine your own conscience, I guess, and do what you feel you have to do."

"And what your family needs you to do, if you have one. Which takes me to something I want to ask you—can you help me get a job in the breaker?"

Owen didn't know if he'd heard right. "You? You're a girl!"

"So you've noticed, have you? And so what? —I can do it. My father's been too ill to go back to work. If I could make just a little money, it would help until he was up again. You said they were short-handed in the breaker."

She tossed the newspaper onto the chair next to her and crossed her arms, waiting.

Owen shook his head and stared. "There's never, ever been a girl working in the breaker that I know of—they wouldn't hire a girl."

"But they'll hire a nine-year-old boy, is that it?" she said.

He thought about it. "Yeah—about as fair as some of the other things they do." He let out a long breath, and swallowed. "Okay, we'll stop by my house and see what kind of work clothes I could loan you. If we bundle you up enough they might not look too close—Morris. Yes, that'll be your new name."

CHAPTER NINE—Vigilantes

The next morning they huddled together outside the breaker building as a steady stream of boys passed through the open doorway and climbed the stairs. A whistle blew for the start of day shift.

"You look grand," Tim said, beaming encouragement at the tattered figure of the new 'boy,' Morris. He was too young to be Maura's suitor, but his open affection for her had always earned him lots of jibes from his mates.

"Come on, we've got to hurry," Owen said. He and Tim rushed Morris up the stairs to the breaker floor, and on up the next flight to the boss' office. They told the boss Morris was Tim's cousin, just arrived from Donegal, and staying at Tim's house. Morris looked a bit more disheveled than most, buried in an overly big canvas shirt, duck hunting cap with earflaps down, shirt collar up, baggy pants, and short rubber boots. The new candidate didn't speak so much as mumble, and just barely peered from under the bill of the hunting cap to meet the boss' glare. Owen told him Morris spoke only Irish, and so there was little attempt made to question him. Morris was hired at a suitably low rate.

Downstairs they gave the same story to anyone that asked. Maura and Tim lived close in a patch of shanties off by themselves, so it was a workable cover. Some of the boys might have recognized Maura, but if so, said nothing. It would be the stuff of legend to outfox the bosses with this dodge. The boys shuffled some willing friends to make a place for Morris between Thomas and Tim, five rows back from Owen and Peter. Owen kept a watch out, but Morris did as well as any boy that had been there a while. Still, he was becoming bruised and tired by lunch break, and they kept him in tight with them when they went down onto the field.

By the time the work shift was over, Morris's hands hurt badly and he drooped. They stopped at the water pump for a drink and a rest, and afterward Owen and Tim accompanied Morris to his shanty to make sure he'd get there.

At his house, Owen and his da took turns washing in the forty gallon galvanized tub in the backyard, and Aine helped with scrubbing their backs. A mineworker got so blackened with coal dust that he had to bathe every day. The soap was homemade, ashes and lime in beeswax, and if it washed well, it near took the freckles off one, also. Liam stood buck-naked for his rinsing, but Owen had his mother set the bucket down and leave before he would stand and rinse himself.

After washing they went in to supper. You'd know they were back at work and could afford decent food again; they sat quietly a few seconds to savor the grand sight of a bowl of kidney stew, nesting potatoes and carrots in a bubbling broth, sitting like a pot of jewels on the table. Liam and Owen fell to it. Aine did not join them, and Owen found himself wondering if she'd sat to meals with the family when Sean was still around.

Liam said little at meals, other than try to answer Owen's questions. Usually Owen wanted to talk about mining, about things Kevin had told him when they explored workings in the old, abandoned mines. Liam had a more limited store of knowledge about the technicalities of mining. He'd always been a laborer, and had advanced no further than tending the ventilating furnace, a big, coal-fired, steel monster set at the bottom of the mineshaft. He could explain to Owen in a general way how his hot furnace sucked dead air out of the mine and exhausted it to the surface through a timber-lined passage in the shaft, called the 'upcast,' and sucked fresh air into the mine through a separate, downcast passage in the shaft. However, Kevin was able to explain to Owen the scientific reason for why the ventilation scheme worked: cold air was heavier and sank naturally into the mine, while the dead air sucked out of the mine tunnels into the furnace became lighter and was pushed up out of the mine. Knowing the mechanics of it fascinated Owen, but he'd never tell his da he'd learned it from Kevin.

Kevin had first gotten to be a miner in one of the few coal mines in Ireland, near Kilkenny, in the south. The English owned the mine, and their work force was mostly English or Welsh miners and Irish laborers. They might make a native Irishman a miner, though, if he'd convert from being a Catholic to a Protestant. The Irish called the ones who did, "soupers." Both Owen and Liam knew that was how Kevin had first become a miner; he'd been a souper, and Liam hated that about him. For Owen, Kevin did what he did and it was for his own conscience to weigh. He thought maybe Kevin just played the English along. One thing he knew for sure: Kevin never went to either church or chapel while living in the mine patch.

When Liam and Owen got home from the mine on Friday evening two men were waiting. They looked like mineworkers, but Owen did not recognize them. Liam went into the house with them, and Owen stayed outside to take his bath. Afterward, he split a rack of firewood and helped Aine tend the oven fire. They kept watching toward the house. It was almost a half-hour before the two men came out and left. Aine brought supper inside and set the table. Liam hardly looked at the plate set in front of him and stared out the window.

Owen started eating, but curiosity soon had him. "What'd those men want?"

Liam turned from the window and looked at him as if he'd just discovered he had company. He shook his head and said, "Some vigilantes raided the Widow Coyle's house, where Jim Tully lived. They were looking for suspected Mollies. Two of Tulley's relatives were shot dead when they resisted, and the Widow was wounded. She died later."

Owen stopped eating and looked at him. "That's terrible. Do they know who any of the vigilantes were?"

Liam was quiet a few seconds. "Their faces were covered, and they wore long cloaks. An old man who boards at the house and works at the livery stables knew a couple of their horses, though. He said one belongs to the butcher, and another to a newcomer in town, a railroad bookkeeper. According to some, the newcomer might also be one of the railroad's Pinkerton Detectives."

"Will the old man tell the police what he saw?"

Liam laughed. "The mine owners' Coal and Iron Police and the Pinkertons work together, so if it's all what it appears to be, nothing would come of his telling. Besides, informing is usually thought a cowardly bargain for seeking favor, and an informer is degraded to the worst of God's creatures. A man will know himself what's to be done with the evidence he owns."

Owen's face flushed. More than once Liam had told him how the English crushed uprisings in Ireland with the help of informers. "Is anything to be done, then?"

"We'd better leave it so," Liam said.

CHAPTER TEN—Tragedy

They met outside Jock's soda shop on Saturday evening. Peter, Thomas, and Owen stood a chance of being served in a beer saloon, but Patrick and Tim would not get by, not as yet. Regardless, Jock was the only possibility for getting any tick from a shop owner till payday. They went in and Jock obligingly drew them five chocolate seltzers. Afterward they hurried to a booth that just emptied and piled in. The shop was a main meeting place in town on Saturday evenings and was considered neutral ground for the various rivalries. All kinds were here tonight, lots of Irish, some Welsh, a few English, and a Cornish lad. Boundaries existed as clear as fence posts between the Irish and the rest.

"There's the whole Welsh breaker crew over to those tables," Peter said. "A couple of them I remember from the bonfire. I wonder if they've patched together their wits yet."

Deak hadn't been at the bonfire, but he'd heard about it. He sat with his shoulders hunched over and glared at them as he said something to his mates. A few turned and gave the Irish table a quick look.

"We'd do well to keep our eyes open when we leave," Thomas said.

The Welsh boys that had been at the bonfire seemed more the lightweights at the table. An encounter with this group might end up a lot more brutal, especially when it included Deak, who'd earned a reputation as one of their nastier faction fighters. A few months ago he'd drubbed one brawny Irish lad that had outweighed him by at least thirty pounds.

The boys glanced at the front door. They were watching for Maura, but she wasn't among the girls who'd just entered. They spoke among themselves for another few minutes, when a fire bell began clanging. They downed their sodas in a single swallow and ran outside the shop.

Smoke billowed high above the buildings a couple of blocks to the north. They ran down to Prescott road and rounded the corner. Flames licked up the sidewall of Roper's hardware and textiles store. A team of horses tied at the railing reared back, overturned their wagon, and dragged it rattling down the street. The boys watched from nearby as the store windows shattered and mountains of flames billowed out.

The Irish volunteer fire company was first to arrive, hurtling around the corner in a tanker wagon drawn by a two-horse team. The firefighters unfurled a canvas hose and ran it out toward the store as two men on the wagon took up positions at the rocker pump. The Welsh volunteer fire company appeared minutes later, and clashed wheel hubs with the Irish wagon as they swerved into position in front of the building. Amid shouts, curses, and laughs, the Welshmen sprang to the ground and ran out their own hoses. While the two companies attacked the blaze, shop owners and workers organized a bucket brigade along the length of the street. A few people watched from the rooftop of a hotel to one side of the burning store.

"Let's see if we can get onto the roof of the lumber warehouse to the other side," Owen said. "We'd have a good look from up there."

They entered the building through the door from a lumberyard out back. No one was inside, and they took the stairs up to the second floor. They found the next stairway behind a clutter of paint cans and building materials toward the rear of the building, and climbed the rickety steps to a closed door at the top. Owen undid the sliding bolt and they stepped out onto the roof. A hot blast of air hit them in the face, and they ran over to the edge of the roof to watch across the alleyway. The second story living quarters were burning now, and some of the upper windows blew out as they watched. The wind was toward them and before long smoke and heat waves forced them back from the roof edge. White streamers of smoke crept over the short parapet wall like giant caterpillars and humped across the roof deck all around them.

"We'd better get out of here before this place goes up, too," Owen yelled. They turned to head down, and froze. Deak and his buddies faced them from the open doorway onto the roof.

"Don't go just yet. You guys like bonfires—remember your little Beltaine picnic? You might try jumping across to the next roof when you're ready to go."

He turned and pushed his buddies down the stairs and slammed the door shut behind him. The boys ran over and pulled at the handle, but couldn't open it; Deak had set the bolt. They hammered and kicked and yelled, but the other boys had gone. They ran to the other side of the roof and looked across the alleyway to the adjacent building. It was wide enough for a wagon team to pass through to the lumberyard, a far distance to leap. The other roof was maybe five or six feet lower—so a running jump might do it. Otherwise, it could be a hard fall onto the cobble-stoned alleyway below.

Tim and Patrick protested it was too far, and they ran back to the door to take turns ramming it with their shoulders. Time and again they tried, and couldn't break through. The tarred roof bubbled and smoked in a couple of places now and they coughed in the rising fumes. A stream of water from a fire hose splashed onto their roof—the fire had probably leaped across and was consuming the building below.

"All right, we can do it—we leap to the next roof," Owen said. "Take a running start, jump up onto that parapet, and push off—let's go!" Everyone stood gaping at him. "Okay, I'll be first—it'll be easy—watch me!"

Owen retreated to the middle of the roof, whispered a prayer, came back running and vaulted off the parapet. A second later he stumbled and fell onto the next roof. He got up and looked back, grinning and waving them on. Black smoke billowed from the upper windows of the warehouse. Next, Peter was in the air, and an instant later skidded flat on his back next to Owen. Thomas and Patrick ran back from view, and seconds later both came up off the parapet, arms and legs flailing in the air. Thomas made it onto the roof, but Patrick was short and threw his arms over the parapet wall as he hit the side. Owen and Peter had him under his shoulders and dragged him up and over. They lined the parapet wall and looked across. Tim stood with arms crossed, hands clasped to his shoulders, looking down at the alleyway and across to his mates.

Flames had broken through the roof now at the front of the warehouse.

"For God's sake, Tim—give a run and jump, do it now!" Owen pleaded.

Tim unfolded his arms and started to turn. A creaking groan rose above all the noise and shouting, then a loud, splintering crack, and Tim was swallowed up

in a burst of sparks and smoke.

The boys got back down to the street and shouted to the firefighters that their friend had been up on the warehouse roof when it collapsed. The firefighters laid on a wall of water with their hoses and sent in a rescue squad. They'd been inside the building too long, and the boys despaired. None of them could look when Tim was carried out on a litter. They couldn't bring themselves to tell anyone about having been out on the roof with him. Their grief and fear of somehow being held responsible shocked and silenced them.

In the early hours of the morning Owen tossed and turned in his bed. The air was muggy and humid and he rose to prop open the hinged window to catch any breeze. Outside the moon set a ghostly glow on the shanties and fences wrapped along the hillside. Accidents and dying were always so near that people in the mine patch got hardened to it, or tried to make themselves that way. The mines snatched away some workers every year, but this hadn't even been a mine accident—and Tim, the youngest of them. Owen lay back down and stared at the shifting reflections of moonlight and shadows slide across the wall. It was such a brutally stupid trick locking them out on the roof. And he'd led his friends into it, getting everyone up there just to watch a fire up close. He covered his eyes and wept.

CHAPTER ELEVEN—The Wake

On Sunday morning Owen listened to Fr. Morrison's remembrance of Tim at Mass. The priest knew his parishioners. He warned them about avoiding the dangerous excesses of wake ceremonies, and how they had no place in the new covenant God had made with his people. The wake in its extremes was a throwback to pagan times, he said. Heads nodded, men sighed, and women wept a little, but Owen knew there'd be no parting with the tradition. There would be a wake for Tim, no matter.

It commenced at Tim's house Monday evening after work. Tim's shanty was that small and his coffin was set on a table pushed against the wall, next to a small window. A bit of moonlight from the window spread across the closed coffin lid. A small bowl of water, floating a few limp, pale yellow blossoms of wild Evening Primrose rested on the lid. The raw pine boards of the coffin had been stained a dark walnut hue and shellacked the night before. It was still tacky to the touch and gave off a sharp, pungent smell. A small, wood kneeler was positioned at the side of the coffin. A planked table of food stretched along another wall of the room and two upended crates covered with cloths stood at either end of the table. One of the makeshift tables held bottles of *poitín*, a cloudy, homebrewed whiskey, along with glasses and cups. The other table held a canister of loose tobacco and a packet of cut papers for hand-rolling cigarettes.

For the first hour there were the spoken remembrances, how Tim had left school at nine years old to work in the breaker and help his family. He had two younger sisters, and a baby brother. When it fell to Owen to say something, what he remembered most and talked about was the stunning voice of Tim. He was ever the soaring alto voice at the hymns and carols before a Christmas Midnight Mass, but he could also sing as bawdy a ballad as known whenever the men invited him into one of their sessions.

The boys' sadness lifted a bit as the evening wore on. This was the first wake where Peter, Thomas, and Owen had been invited to sip whiskey. The custom was that when the bottle and a cup were set before you, you were expected to offer something for the wake—a song, a story, maybe a poem. Owen wasn't much of a singer, but he had a few good poems. Some he'd learned from Liam, others he'd gotten from Kevin's shelf of books. On impulse he recited *The Shortcut to the Rosses. A* traveler becomes enchanted when he hears piping music along a pathway, meets a faerie woman, and falls in love with her. When he awakens from the spell, he's alone, and his heart has been taken and replaced with one of stone. A heart of stone was exactly how Owen felt, unable to forgive himself for Tim.

Peter and Thomas sang ballads in *sean-nos*, an unaccompanied singing style that almost everyone used, and they alternated Irish verses with the English. Only recent arrivals of older, rural folks, from places in the west like Donegal or Mayo, preferred to stay in the Irish altogether when singing or talking.

Owen saw Maura standing against a wall watching him as he recited another poem. After he finished he went over to her.

"Come and join in," he said, taking her arm. "No need being so shy." He'd had a few sips by now, and his tongue was slow getting out of its way.

"Well, I was never shy," she said, "But the wake for Tim has put an awful mood on me. All right, I'll do something. It might strike some as bold, but no matter; It'll be breaking up soon and I'll be joining the women in the keening."

"You—keening—since when? You're not yet old enough."

"Aren't I? Well the women have asked me." She pulled her arm away and walked over to take a chair, signaling Peter to pass her the cup. She but touched her lips to the brim and set it on the floor before her. In a high, plaintive voice she sang *The Song of Renvyle*, about a spirited young woman who ploughs her own fields and builds her own house on Ireland's western shore, and waits for her true love to find her. Maura finished with:

I've poked a fire for all of the night while the moon slipped away

Oh, if only a true love could have found a way to my door

But Mother Mary and dear Christ I'm alone again at the dawn

With the cocks crowing and all in Renvyle asleep but me

Maura got a rousing hand and she looked over at Owen and winked. She'd no sooner risen from her chair than the women gathered together in front of the coffin. Mrs. Donnelly and a couple of relatives took to the kneeler and the other women and Maura knelt on the floor behind them. It was time to take leave of Tim. The men got up from chairs and from sitting on the floor against the wall, and with the boys following went outside. The keening started low at first, with the lamentations scattered and separately called, almost unrecognizable as human voices what with the grief in them. A wind coursed through the trees and the men moved together in tighter clusters. The boys stood together, off by themselves. The keening became higher-pitched and more otherworldly, rising and falling against the steady drone of the wind through the treetops. On and on it went, forever.

Owen thought in a confused way about how the Molly Maguires surely wouldn't let any brute injustice go unanswered. Well, that was altogether different, but the wasting of Tim's life wanted something from them, at least something. He became more morose and finally decided that, yes, something was needed, and he would be the one for it.

"Tomorrow I'll get Deak for what he's done," he said to his mates.

They stared at him, and all flinched when a piercing shriek and lamentation overrode the awful wailing. The keening continued but grew lower.

Peter said, "Tomorrow it is, then, on the field at lunch break. The rest of the Welsh aren't likely to stay out of it and we're only the four, but probably we can count on others of our lads jumping in to help."

Owen said, "No, just me. There'd be a lot of boys discharged from work over a faction fight like that. Tomorrow morning I'm going to slip back to where he's working and lay into him right there. We can settle it pretty quick, and only risk the two of us getting fired."

"No, you can't do that," Peter said. "The two back benches are all Welsh, and it's only a few feet to the end of the chutes. They'll have you beaten-up and flung into the hoppers before we could help. Wait till the break."

Owen said no more. He knew what he had to do.

He waited for Maura to come out from the keening. She looked drawn and tired when she came through the doorway. He nodded to her and they walked together along the pathway. They spoke hardly a word until they were at the lane below her shanty. Pausing there, Owen told her what he planned to do the next day.

She rolled her eyes and blew a sharp breath. "But you'll get fired, and you could get hurt fighting around those coal chutes and contraptions in there—and for what? It'll do Tim no good at all. Give it up and let Deak's conscience destroy him for what he did."

"They say anyone who doesn't repay an injustice deserves to suffer more of the same."

"Probably what the Mollies told Jim Tully when they sent him against the blacklegs. Look at the outcome of that."

"I can't turn away from what I have to do."

"Don't you do this, Owen. I have a bad feeling about it. You'll have me keening at your own wake, next."

CHAPTER TWELVE—Breaker Fight

The next morning Owen waited near the pump engine shed. Across the way railcars were filling with coal from the hoppers at the end of the breaker building. As soon as one car filled the train rolled ahead, stopped, and more coal thundered from the overhead hopper into the empty car below. It was an hour after starting time for the breaker, and by now the boys inside felt the dull monotony of cleaning coal. He'd have surprise on his side, calling Deak out without any sign or warning. He'd make him regret trapping Tim on that roof, but he had to be quick. His lad was tough as a mine mule, and if he didn't blow him out in the first couple of minutes, Deak might have him. Owen waited until the last car finished loading and the train pulled away. He stayed in the shadows while the brakeman reset the switch, waited a few minutes till he was gone, and hurried over to the breaker. Time to move in and get it done.

The rickety building vibrated and swayed to the pulse of the machinery as he climbed the stairs. At the top of the second flight he entered the doorway and looked up at the rows and rows of boys at work. The grinding and bucking of the massive coal breakers at the top of the chutes set his own legs to shaking as he let the door snap shut behind him.

For a few seconds he stood motionless, gathering his nerve, then moved up the walking beam until he drew opposite the back row of boys. Heavy clouds of coal dust swirled above the chutes and he craned his neck straining to see the faces of boys seated along the bench. Deak usually sat at the second chute over, but he couldn't be sure it was him. Wouldn't it be a great pity if he'd missed coming to work after all? Owen stayed still as a post, not wanting to draw attention. Finally, the boy turned to laugh at his mate beside him; yes, it was Deak. Owen gathered himself for the rush out—and someone grabbed at his arm.

He flailed loose from the clutching hand as he spun about, and Morris cried out as he lost his balance. Shocked, Owen tried to catch him but he toppled from the beam onto the coal chute beside them. Morris stumbled getting to his feet on the sliding bed of coal, and fell over into the next chute. Deak stuck his foot out to stop him from sliding beneath the bench atop the coal, but in his struggle to get up, Morris fell again and slipped under the bench. Owen leaped down and plunged and stumbled across the coal chutes. Desperately grabbing Deak's foot for anchorage, he went under the bench and caught Morris's ankle. The loud thunder of coal falling into the gaping hopper just ahead drowned out all the shouting, while Deak held on desperately, both arms wrapped around the bench.

Deak, Maura and Owen stood before the breaker boss in his office on the balcony. Maura's blackened face was streaked white where the tears had run down her cheeks. Her cap was gone and her hair splayed out over her shoulders and back. The boss's forehead wrinkled and his eyes bulged.

"What in the infernal hell happened down there? And you," he sputtered and his mouth opened and shut a few times before he got any words out. "You—Morris! What in God's creation are you all about?" He thrust out his switch and lifted a curtain of hair from her shoulder.

Maura's chin trembled. "I'm a girl, Sir, but it hasn't caused a bit of trouble with picking the slate."

"Don't act smart with me—you wouldn't be flopping onto a coal chute if you had any wits about you. I don't know what's going on around here, but you're fired!" he shouted. "You're lucky you weren't loaded into a railroad car and on your way to Philadelphia

71

by now. Get out of here quick before the super sees you, and you two, Williams, Dougherty, get yourselves back to work. Do we need to put on a bloody circus going about plucking idjits off coal chutes?"

Owen was still shaken by the events, but he kept an eye on Deak as they went down the stairs from the balcony. Deak looked just as dazed. Well, Owen thought, he'd have to leave things where they lay; there'd been enough trouble. Maura gave a tug to his sleeve when they reached the chute floor, and she kept going toward the door. Owen caught up.

"I'm sorry, Maura. I know you worried about what might happen. It looks like the only thing I've managed to do was to get you fired."

She swallowed and nodded. "See if you can find me another job," she said, and left.

After work Owen and his father walked for home together, until they reached the AOH lodge. Some mine workers waited outside and they motioned Liam toward the lodge entrance. Owen knew a few of them, but they had other things on their minds and no one smiled or waved to him. As soon as Liam went inside the men followed after him.

Owen ate supper at home, and later climbed the hill to Kevin's place. He looked around the room anxiously when Kevin let him in. Maura wasn't there; most likely she was at home, dejected about being fired from her job. He felt miserable and told Kevin the whole, sorry story. Kevin swallowed a few rumbling coughs as he listened, and then got up to walk about and cough some more. He sat at the table again and drummed his fingers.

"How'd you expect that would make anything right?"

Owen shrugged. "I don't know. Tim's death had me crazy."

"You're getting to be as reckless as your da. And I've heard things that puts him in the thick of some pretty desperate business around here."

Owen's nerves had eased a little, but now they roiled up again. One thing, and one thing only, flew to mind. "You don't mean Molly Maguire business?"

"Yes, I'd say that was it."

"But we don't know that much about them, and maybe the Mollies are needed to stand up for the mine workers now that the union is busted—right?"

"They're ignorant men if they think the killings of a few mine bosses are going to frighten anyone in the railroad. Losing a few people at the bottom rung of the enterprise is just a cost of doing business until they can crush the Mollies, like they did the union."

If Kevin suspected da, did others? Owen was horrified to think about the killings, especially if his da was one of the Mollies and they did it. If only it would all end, and soon.

CHAPTER THIRTEEN—Underground Promotion

In the days afterward, the tragedy of Tim's death continued to weigh on Owen, but now, whenever he encountered Deak at work or in town, a silent truce held between them.

Meanwhile the Railroad was far from calling any truce with their rebellious workers, and on top of crushing new wage cuts, added work rules were introduced and higher coal production quotas were set. Without a union the workers felt powerless to resist, and then a new wave of "coffin" notices went out to the mine bosses from the Molly Maguires. In response, the Railroad increased the ranks of their Coal and Iron Police and hired more Pinkerton Detectives.

In the week following Owen's set-to with Deak, the breaker boys were on lunch break playing ball on the field next to the breaker, when a din of shouts caught everyone's attention. The boys stopped playing and watched a large crowd of men approach from the road.

"Looks like mine workers," Peter said. "So many of them—they must be from all the mines between here and Shamokin."

Owen watched and thought of the men who'd called his da inside the lodge earlier in the week. Maybe they had let him know something like this was coming. When the men reached the breaker some of them went to the shaft head and rode the lift down to the mine level. One of the newcomers, a bearded, bulbous-nosed man, called the breaker boys together on the field. He told them workers at his mine had been fired for breaking the new work rules set by the railroad. They were calling out all the mineworkers everywhere to join their strike, and they wanted the Hopmore Mine, men and boys, both, to come along and help shut down every mine in the county.

Shortly, the lift began bringing up the Hopmore workers from underground. Liam was one of the first to come up and join the strikers, and the breaker boys walked over to form up alongside the ranks of men. Owen felt proud they'd been asked to join the men.

Before the strikers could start along the road to the next mine a dozen horsemen and three wagonloads of men came from the direction of town. The mounted men cantered smartly across the field. Their riders wore the forest green uniform and silver badge of the Coal and Iron Police, and they formed up in front of the mineworkers. The wagons rolled up behind them and men with rifles jumped down. They wore everyday clothes—townsmen—and had silver deputy badges pinned to their jackets. The mineworkers backed away from the line of horsemen and shouted curses at them.

"Break up this mob, and those of you who are employed here get back to work," shouted a sergeant of the horsemen.

No one moved, and the horsemen slid long, dark batons from their belts. The mineworkers began a rumbling murmur as they drew farther back, and some began throwing stones at the advancing horsemen. The riders spurred their mounts ahead, swinging batons, and the workers broke ranks. Some men darted past the horsemen and rushed at the line of plainclothes deputies in the rear. Townsmen at a far end of the line opened fire, and mineworkers crumpled to the ground.

The breaker boys fled beneath the conveyor belts to the waste piles. The sergeant blew a whistle and shouted for the deputies to cease-fire. The panicked deputies backed away from the regrouping miners, but held their rifles at the ready. The horsemen reformed ranks and charged the workers, slashing left and right with batons. The breaker boys ran farther back, beneath trestle towers deeper in the culm piles where they couldn't be reached on horseback. The police opened up with volleys of pistol fire, and the mineworkers broke and fled in all directions.

The boys climbed the towers and watched in horror as more workers were clubbed to the ground. Some men who had been wounded in the initial fusillade struggled to their feet. A few boys recognized fathers or relatives among the wounded, and leaped from the towers to run to their aid. Owen caught glimpses of his da marshalling dazed workers together in the cover of cable drums and scaffolding near the shaft head. His heart hammered and he barely breathed until the police, their fury spent, pulled back to reform their ranks. They allowed the wounded to be carried from the field, and watched until the remaining miners went back to work.

Back inside the breaker, Owen thought about the havoc. He had taken part in some early demonstrations during the Long Strike, but the union had controlled those fairly well. They hadn't let violence take hold as happened today. He was still shaken, but his biggest worry was lifted when he spotted his da going back to work after the strikers were subdued. A blessed mercy, that, and he'd take it.

The breaker boss was called away for most of the afternoon and was in a fearful rage when he got back. He laid his switch on a few shoulders as he walked about the beams. He'd already been shorthanded, and now boys whose fathers had been shot or badly injured had left work. Owen was startled when the boss swatted his arm with the switch and motioned him up to his office. The boss swatted Peter on the back and ordered him upstairs, too. The boys followed him along the chutes as he whacked Deak, and a boy next to him, and pointed them upstairs, too.

They crowded into the cubbyhole office and the boss closed the door so that something less than a shout might be heard above the pounding breakers.

"They want two boys from our breaker transferred underground," he said.

In spite of all the terrible things that had happened today, Owen's heart leapt. He nudged Peter, who looked like the angel Gabriel had just spoken. Pink-lipped smiles spread across the blackened faces of Deak and his friend. The boss had mentioned only two jobs, thought Owen, so why were we all up here?

The boss tapped with his switch, "Where might you run into blackdamp, Dougherty?"

Owen was startled, but he'd learned the mining gases from Kevin, and made efforts to pass along that knowledge to Peter. "Low areas, Sir, maybe in where there'd been no clean air moving past for some time."

He turned from Owen to Peter. "Mightn't it blow up if you struck a match in it, Reilly?" he asked.

Peter's face pinched while he scratched his jaw. He glanced at Owen, and saw him frown. "Not at all, Sir," Peter blurted.

The boss sniffed. He stared at Peter a few seconds and turned to the Welsh boy standing alongside him. "How about stinkdamp—that stuff liable to blow up on you?" he said.

The boy swallowed hard and replied, "Yessir—indeed it might, Sir."

The boss swatted the boy's leg hard. "Muddling Idjit." He pointed the switch at Deak. "What gas'll blow you to hell, Williams?" he shouted.

Deak hollered out, "Firedamp, Sir."

The boss's lip curled, he wheeled to Peter again, and thrust his face next to his. "Is this a fact, Reilly?"

Peter leaned back, his jaw going, unable to see past the boss to

Owen, and not knowing the answer anymore than he could recite the Seven Deadly Sins for Fr. Morrisey. "It is, Sir," he stammered.

The boss spun away. He stood with his back to them, watching through the office window to the breaker floor below. "Have a go at another, Reilly; what'll make you as lightheaded as a sodden Paddy drunk on the *poitín*?" he said.

Peter's brow crumpled and he stole a glance to Owen standing with hand to chin, smiling, tapping a soot-blackened finger against glistening white teeth.

"Whitedamp, that's what it is, Sir," Peter said, almost giddy with the relief of it.

The boss muttered and was quiet a few seconds. "Dougherty and Williams get down to the shaft head and wait there for the mine boss. The rest of you get back downstairs to your benches."

Peter's chin dropped to his chest. Owen winced at his friend's disappointment. Three right to Deak's one, and still Peter was passed over. Maybe the only wonder was that the boss gave one Paddy his chance to go underground. The boys started down the stairs together. Owen nudged his friend, "He saw you know your stuff. This isn't all the new help they need underground. You'll be down too, next week." Peter was too dejected to say anything.

CHAPTER FOURTEEN—Mule Driver

The mine boss handed Owen a brass tag from a box on the table. Each miner hung his personal tag on the safety board in the shaft house before he went down to begin a shift. Owen's tag, #189, had a thumb-polished finish, and the etched digits had been nearly rubbed away. He hoped that meant the former owner had enjoyed a long career underground. He smiled as he polished it with his own thumb, and thought he might like to cement a pin on the back and wear it into town. Next stop, the storehouse, where a laborer found him a pair of gumboots and a tin oil lamp for his cap. Used equipment, for sure, but marvelous to possess. Afterward the mine boss took Owen and Deak for the trip down the shaft to get them a work assignment. It was the first time Owen had been underground at Hopmore No. 7, but he knew it to be similar to two of the abandoned mines he'd explored with Kevin—only much deeper and bigger.

Two parallel tunnels connected all parts of the mine with the shaft.

Stretched out ahead of them as they left the shaft cage was one called the gangway, feeding fresh air into the mine and laid with steel tracks to carry coal carts to and from the workings ahead. A few steps farther along and they exited the gangway and went through a wooden door opening into the adjacent tunnel, called the airway, used to collect and return stale air from all the distant mining chambers.

The mine boss stopped and tapped Liam on the back until he paused shoveling coal to the ventilating furnace. Liam's face brightened when he turned and saw his son, and he flashed a thumbs-up before giving full attention to the boss. Owen barely heard the boss tell Liam about the promotion underground, while Owen thought about his da's lonely sort of working life. He felt the damp air sucked from the mine rushing past him into the open, flame-belching maw of the furnace. The superheated air roared and shook the metal plates as it expanded inside the fiery iron monster, and rose through the shaft to exhaust at ground level. A feeling almost of despair smote Owen as he thought of the years his da had held to such a mute, brutal job.

Afterward he and Deak followed behind the mine boss, slogging along the black, mucky floor of the airway. They went in a ways and stopped at one of the chambers being mined off to one side. Each chamber was driven with a breasting about thirty feet wide, and the coal seam being mined stood about five-and-a-half feet high. The shallow height kept workers in the chamber stooped over as they mined out the seam with their picks. The seam bed pitched upward at a slight grade going in, so that the men worked continually uphill. The boss went to talk with the men in the chamber, and a few minutes later came back out.

"Williams—I'm leaving you off here. You'll be helping the miner's assistant fill the mine cars and be giving a hand in the chamber wherever you're needed." Deak was elated. He was being jumped up a couple of notches to a chamber laborer, right off the mark. Owen was envious.

The mine boss led Owen into a cross heading leading back to the gangway tunnel. A boy sat by a timbered brattice, and he jumped up from his seat to open a door for them. A strong draft of air funneled through the doorway. The mine boss rubbed his chin as he paused to study the boy. His job was to assist the loaded mine cars through on their way to the shaft. He looked young, and Owen was dejected at the thought of being assigned this dull job while the boy was moved up. Becoming a skilled miner suddenly seemed a long way off. But the mine boss abruptly turned away and continued through the doorway. The boy's hopes were dashed, and he stared after Owen rushing to follow the boss.

Entering the gangway, they turned back toward the shaft and slogged through mud alongside the steel tracks. When they reached a timbered stable near the shaft, the boss paused to watch a boy adjusting a harness on a team of mules. The boss stood with hands on hips and looked about. He nodded at the mule driver and said, "Take Dougherty here under your wing for the rest of the day, and show him what's to be done. You can start as labor assistant up at Chamber Twelve tomorrow."

"Yes Sir," The boy blinked and struggled to keep a sober look. As soon as the boss turned and left them, the boy let out a long breath and shook his head, as if not quite able to believe his good fortune. Owen was a bit relieved, too; a mule driver wasn't the best job he could have hoped for, but it wasn't the worst, either. The boy was Welsh, near the same age as Owen, but he wasn't interested in being friendly and didn't talk much. He showed Owen how to hook the mules to a train of mine cars, and led him through some routine work trips.

They loaded mine cars with timber props, roof supports, and other supplies brought down the shaft and transported them back to the mining chambers, then pulled cars loaded with coal back out to the shaft. The mules were calm, uncomplaining workers, and as much as the boy snapped impatiently at them with his long, snaking whip, the mules moved at their own pace. That evening the boy showed Owen how to peel the leads and tracers from the mules, rub them down, feed them, and do what was needed around the stable. At the whistle for quitting time, Owen lagged behind, leaning against the side of the stall, and watched his charges eat hay from the trough. Poor duffers, they'd be down here all their lives without ever seeing daylight again. There was still a long ways to go to be a skilled miner, but he was on the way at last.

Owen met with his mates when he came up from the mine at the end of his shift, and gave them a glowing picture of his new job. Afterward he waited for Liam to dress the coal blanket, bank the furnace, and come up from the mine. He couldn't wipe the grin from his face when he saw his da walk from the lift, and went up to shake hands with him. Liam clapped him on the back and they set off for town. Going through the entry gate Liam spotted a fresh notice on one of the posts. They stopped and looked at it—a new blacklist of six men, identified as the main troublemakers who had tried to strike the mines that day. Two of the names were from the Hopmore No. 7 mine; the rest were from mines over Shamokin way. They talked quietly about the notice. Liam spat on the ground and they started down the road. When they reached the AOH lodge Liam took Owen inside.

"Pull a couple of tall ones for the lad and myself," Liam said to the barkeep. "We've got a new underground man here. He left his working mates, the mules, outside."

Owen smiled, and when the barkeep pushed the glass across the counter he took a long swallow through the sudsy top. "Will I be able to join the lodge now?" he asked his da.

"I'll put your name in," Liam said. "Likely they'll take you in before the end of the year."

Four workers came up to the bar and talked in low voices with Liam. Two of them wore head wrappings. Owen recalled seeing one of them go down in a police baton charge. Liam's face looked tired and worn when he told Owen he'd see him at home, but he'd be late. He went with the men to the meeting room at the rear of the lodge.

Owen worried about a Mollies' response to the shootings and blacklist. He hadn't known any of the men that had been shot, but there'd be some grief in a few households that night. Just as bad, if a man couldn't work anymore he and his family would be on charity, or what charity might be available around the mine patch—relatives, or the Church, maybe. He stared at his reflection in the bar mirror. Things were getting worse. He put down the unfinished glass and left.

At home, while he bathed in the tub, Owen told Aine about the attempt to strike the mine, and the shootings. She stopped scrubbing his back.

"But da's okay; he went back to work after it was over. He'll be home a little late, though. Some men at the lodge wanted to talk with him."

Aine brought more water into the yard for him to rinse, and went back out to the stove. He called out; "I finally got out of the breaker, mom—got promoted to underground. I drive a team of mules in the mine, and it won't be long now till I get to be a skilled miner and out on my own."

He toweled off, dressed, and went into the house to wait for her to bring in supper. He was at the table for a while, and when she didn't come in he went out to see what was the matter. She sat on a stool near the stove, leaning over, arms resting across her knees. She looked up when he came to stand beside her, shook her head, and stared again at the licking flames. Owen pulled up a stool and sat beside her. He watched her, waiting for her to tell him what might be bothering her. Her hair was loose, lifting a little in the breeze. She had a nice, wide mouth, and if she'd relax it she'd be even grander looking. She clasped and unclasped her hands and looked out over the hollows and ridges. Dusk was settling in and the ridges took on a purple hue.

"When you leave I'll be going back to live with my sister in Ireland," she said.

If he'd been hit in the back with a maul it mightn't have jarred him as much. He sat up straight and folded his arms across his chest, more to cover his heartbeat than anything else. When he thought he might have control of his voice he asked, "What about da?"

"I don't want to live with him anymore."

The breeze fell off and a pair of owls called to one another from some trees beyond. He took a few deep breaths and steadied himself. "Did something happen?"

"My life can't go on like this. I'd thought long ago of leaving, after he'd sent Sean off with Ben, and later getting back that dreadful news of their loss. But I stayed and tried hard to overcome my anger and grief, and accept things as they were. Now even that's become impossible."

Sean—he was always going to be there. He just was. "Why has it become impossible now?" Owen said.

"Because of what he's doing. Because he's become one of those hard, brutal men—a Molly Maguire."

"He told you this?"

She nodded. "He tries to make it right to himself and to me, the nights he comes home after one of the assassinations. He doesn't say, but perhaps he'd been the one who did it. Maybe in time it becomes as easy as singing a young boy off to war."

"Boys," Owen said. "Ben and Sean." It startled him to realize he'd said it.

Aine looked at him and blinked. She got up from the stool, picked up his supper plate from the stove shelf, and carried it inside. He watched as she came back out, threw a shawl over her shoulders, and took the pathway up to the refuge. He called to her but she kept going.

CHAPTER FIFTEEN—More Assassinations

That evening Owen was late getting to the confraternity meeting at the church hall. Peter had saved a seat and moved over to give him the chair on the aisle. Fr. Morrison was already into his talk on the Good Shepherd, and how he knows all his sheep and takes care of them, and how the Church is God's shepherd on earth.

Owen slumped in his chair and looked distractedly about the hall. A painting of the Archbishop of Philadelphia hung on the wall; the bishop dressed in a jeweled, mitered hat, and carrying a gold, curly-ended shepherd's crook. Maybe it's no wonder he warned them against the Molly Maguires. He wanted to hold sway over some docile sheep, and the Mollies weren't like that—they were hard men.

After the lecture they helped pick up the chairs and made a bit of room for dancing. While they waited for a pair of musicians to arrive, Peter, Thomas, and Patrick gathered around to hear more of Owen's first day underground. Peter got so depressed afterward that Owen took up touch boxing with him to jolt him out of his dismal mood. Fr. Morrison came by and broke up the roughhousing. He put an arm around Owen's shoulder and led him off to a quiet corner.

"Owen, I was terribly disappointed your mother didn't make it to Tim's funeral Mass, or to the burial service. She came here as a girl in the same year as Tim's mother, they were friends, and your mother was a very devout girl at the time." He turned Owen to face him and held both his shoulders. "Isn't it time we tried to get her to Sunday Mass again? I know what troubles her, but the war and your brothers' deaths are years gone, now. It's not good what she's doing. She needs God and his sacraments more than ever in these terrible times."

"I don't know what I can do about that," Owen said. "She won't talk about the Church or God, now. Not anymore."

The intent look on Fr. Morrison's face faded to sadness. "She could be such an inspiration to your da, and perhaps turn him away from the evil society in which he's enmeshed. You know of what I'm speaking?"

Owen swallowed, and said nothing.

The priest shook his head and dropped his hands from Owen's

shoulders. "Do not mistake pride and arrogance for bravery, Owen, not even for the sake of your da. Faith and humility are the swords by which we shall conquer adversities in this life." He tapped him on the arm and turned away.

Maura came over after Fr. Morrison left. The dancing had begun, but Owen needed some air. "Will you come with me outside?" he said.

Maura nodded and they went out to the rear yard of the church. There was enough of a moon to see lights and darks in the flowerbeds, but no color. The ground rose toward the rear of the yard, rising up to the graveyard at the hilltop. They walked up together. Tim's casket had been carried along this pathway right after the Requiem Mass. His uncle had wanted to pipe him up to the gravesite, but Fr. Morrison would have no barbaric war pipes at a church service. They sat on the ground next to Tim's headstone, sawed and chiseled by a miner from the local limestone. He'd done a fair job of chiseling out the inscription. Owen traced the letters with a finger: *Timothy Óg Donnelly—the young Timothy Donnelly—* and indeed, not only the youngest of the Donnelly's; the youngest of the friends' he was. He read aloud the dates marked, *1862 – 1875,* and remembered Ben had served as godfather at Tim's Baptism, just before Ben left with Sean to join the fateful Irish

Brigade. The final inscription chiseled to the stone was *Slán Abhaile*—Safe Home.

Owen told Maura of his promotion underground. She gave a shout and pinned him, holding his arms to the ground and leaned over him, laughing. "There'll be no shutting you up now; you'll be insufferable," she said.

"I can't hear you. Lie down a little tighter to me."

She swatted his head and they sat up, grinning.

Owen pulled up a handful of sedge and tore pieces of it to cast into the breeze as he watched her. Tweedy-limbed girl, but limber as a wagon spring. He wondered what it might be like to one day sleep with her, and then put the thought away when he remembered what place they were in. He slid over closer to her and they watched the sky, the millions of glittering stars, and listened to the breeze winnow through tall stands of sedge.

Owen said, "My mom will leave da and go back to live with her sister in Ireland as soon as I'm on my own."

Maura stifled a cry and laid a hand on his arm. "Why? I have never even heard you say they've fought."

"They don't much, but she's always blamed him for Sean, and now she told me he's admitted being a Molly Maguire. She thinks maybe he's been involved in some of the assassinations, and I guess that's finished everything for her."

"The Mollies—that must be frightening, and the both of you knowing that. Are you angry with her for thinking to leave?"

"No, not angry. Miserable, but not angry. Even if she left da I don't know why she's got to go clear over there. I'd always take care of her here."

They were both silent. After a while Maura asked, "Do you still pray?"

Owen turned to her, wishing he could see her face more clearly in the dim starlight. It felt a sort of weakness to admit it, but he said, "Yes, sometimes."

That night Liam came home very late. Owen glanced out his window and saw a comet fall in the predawn light. He listened to their voices, low, sometimes strained and quickly spoken, then long pauses. After a while, silence. Sometime later, Liam's footsteps echoed through the house, and he was gone.

In the morning Aine shook Owen awake and before he could rise up on an elbow she was away from his room and out of the house. He dressed and went outside, doused his face in a basin of cold water, and dried off. Aine hurried past with a tea mug and a plate of food. He followed her inside and sat down to breakfast.

"Am I late?" he said.

"No. Take your da's lunch pail along with you. He'll be at work, or in jail, one or the other."

He stopped sawing sausage with his fork. "What happened?"

"Something went wrong last night, as if anything was ever right to begin with. Two men were shot, and later some friends of your da were arrested and taken from their homes by the railroad police."

She stood with elbows bent, fists tucked into her sides, and stared out the open doorway at thunderheads moving across the hills from the east.

"What were the shootings about—did he tell you?"

"The shot men were mine bosses, one here, one over to Shamokin. Your da was furious that the boss at Shamokin had been robbed, too, as if that was the biggest shame to what was done."

CHAPTER SIXTEEN—Miner's Craft

After going down in the shaft lift that morning, Owen hurried through the door to the airway and on to the furnace. Liam stopped shoveling coal and nodded as Owen set the lunch pail down next to his jacket.

"Is everything going to be all right, da? I heard you come in late last night, and Mom said this morning that there'd been trouble."

Liam dragged his sleeve across a sweaty brow. The air around them seemed to pulse as the huge furnace rumbled and the steel plates clicked rapidly with the rising heat. "She told you that, did she? Yes, well, it seems a few Mollies might have shamed the rest. From what I heard a couple of mine bosses got what they deserved, including our own outside boss, Mr. Powell. The ugly part is that the Shamokin boss was robbed, too, and if any Molly stooped to such thievery, I've no use for the man."

Liam looked over at other mine workers coming through the doorway. "It's not the sort of thing we can safely speak of here. Men love justice and fraternity, but hard times can test their honor. Weak men become thieves, and the worst of men become informers." Liam touched Owen on the shoulder and went back to shoveling coal.

Owen wished he'd have said things were going to work out, no matter what—something to hope for. He went back through the door and hurried along the gangway to the stables.

The harness and traces were still new to him and he hung everything on the wall to go over the setup and the fastenings. Another boy led his team of mules past and hurried away down the gangway. When Sarah had been dressed out to the best of his memory, he ran his hand along her chest and flanks, tugging at each strap and binding. Maybe he hadn't leapt through it all, but he'd managed to get a snug fit-up. He brought out the other mule, Elsie, fitted her out behind Sarah, and stepped back to inspect his work. Not bad, they were at least headed in the same direction.

A string of empty mining carts pulled by one of the other teams rolled past, headed toward the mining chambers. Owen hurried his team in the opposite direction, to make his pickup at the shaft. The lift had just brought down empty carts from the breaker, and some mining supplies marked for chamber eight. A mine laborer helped

Owen wheel three carts out onto the tracks, and while the laborer coupled them, Owen hooked up the mule traces. He climbed up at the front of the carts, cracked his whip, and began the day.

Black seepage water trickled past along both sides of the tracks as they went up a slight grade. He had to constantly watch the headroom in places where the roof rock sagged, or where crossbeams bowed down into the tunnel opening. His mining lamp didn't illuminate very far ahead, and after a few knocks on the head, he noticed how the mules used their long ears to feel along the roof, and so he'd duck low whenever he saw their heads dip.

Everywhere water trickled down from roof joints and sheared rock zones. At some places the floor rock had heaved, and in other places it had settled so that the mules had to splash through standing pools of water. Owen counted each crosscut tunnel he passed, until he reached the crosscut for chamber eight. He switched the carts onto the crosscut tracks, and traveled through toward the mining chamber.

Inside the chamber three figures were silhouetted against the dim glow of miner's lamps against a distant coal face. Owen pulled his carts close to some broken piles of coal and unhitched the mule traces. Two of the figures came forward to meet him. They were less than a few feet away before he made out the faces beneath their lamps—Deak, and a miner's assistant, Elis.

"Did you bring our props?" Elis asked. Owen nodded toward one of the carts. "Well, what are you waiting for? You and Deak get busy unloading them."

It wasn't Owen's job. He needed to leave these, get more carts at the shaft, and bring them back to other chambers, but he shrugged and worked with Deak to lift out the heavy timber props. Elis sat on a coal pile, pulled a cigarette stub from his shirt pocket, and lit up.

They were unloading the last prop when the old miner approached from the face. He counted the props and looked through the empty carts. He said to Elis, "You can start drilling the face where I've marked it. I'll be going back to the shaft and see if they've sent any blasting powder down."

"Right you are, Martin." Elis got up and nipped out his cigarette.

"I saw a powder keg in the lift when I took out the props," Owen said to the miner. "I could measure out your powder and bring it back in on my next trip." He glanced past Martin at the coal face. "Is it about forty pounds you'd be shooting today, Sir?"

Elis went rigid, while Martin rubbed his jaw and studied Owen. It was a bold guess, prompted by things Kevin had taught him on their trips to the old, abandoned mines.

"'Bout that, Martin said, "if you were shooting it as fine as usual. But they're making us pay for our own powder these days, and counting only heaped carts for full pay, so I've been shooting the face a little coarser. Uses less powder and the coal bulks up higher in the carts. Bring me in about thirty pounds. What's your name?"

"Owen Dougherty."

"Pity," he said, meaning Owen had to be Irish. "All right, let's get on with our work." Martin turned and headed back up to the coal face.

"Be right there, Martin," Elis said. "I'll quick help Deak load up a few of these big coal pieces in a cart."

Owen took hold of Sarah's reins and walked ahead to lead the mules from the chamber. Elis sprang, clamping a hand over Owen's mouth and twisting his arm up behind his back. He shoved Owen hard against the side of the coal pillar and hissed in his ear, "You cheeky, Paddy bastard. Don't you ever say anything to any miner I'm working for, except Yes Sir and No Sir, not ever again. Do you understand me, you cod?"

Owen tried to turn but Elis twisted his arm tighter. Elis' breath stank and Owen twisted his face away. Elis gave another jerk to his arm making Owen see lightning and then shoved him free. Owen staggered back against the pillar; his legs trembled and his breath came in quick gasps. He stared at Elis, a bigger guy, probably in his twenties, and anyway Owen's arm felt useless, almost yanked out of its socket. Elis spat at Owen's feet and walked away. Deak stood quietly at a distance, watching. Owen pushed off from the pillar, took Sarah's reins, and left the chamber.

CHAPTER SEVENTEEN—The Sprag Boy

The run-in with Elis sobered Owen. Working underground was every bit as exciting as he'd imagined, but he had to remember how bad the jostling got over job status down here. He continued hauling supplies from the shaft back to the chambers, and later that morning, after the miners blasted down another face, the new loads of coal were ready to take out. He checked Martin's cartloads—a lot more empty spaces amongst bigger chunks of coal. The crafty old devil would fill more carts in a day's work, and there wouldn't be any more actual coal mined than before. Even after paying for the powder, he might not lose a penny in pay. Probably get a laugh out of Kevin, who might have thought of doing exactly the same thing.

The run back to the shaft with loaded carts took a lot of attention. The tracks were a smooth downhill most of the way, but some of the weaker rock had shifted as time passed. In those sections the tracks buckled and tilted every which way, so that the mules had to pull hard to get across. When the carts got back onto a smooth grade, the driver had to hold his mules back to keep a loaded train under control. Sprag boys waited along steep track sections, and if a driver lost control and the train got rolling fast enough to maybe overturn, the boy ran alongside and jammed a sprag, or stick, into the wheel spokes. The sprag would whip up against the bottom of the cart, locking the wheel, and slowing the train.

One of the sprag boys was stationed at 'Slick Grade,' a steep section of rail coming off a long, heaved-up section of ground. Twice that morning Owen had pulled back too late, or the mules had been too frisky coming onto Slick Grade, and he'd lost control. The kid had materialized out of the darkness each time, a slight whippet of a lad with a tattered long shirt and galoshes six sizes too big, running and splashing alongside the train. With just a frantic nod from Owen, the kid would go for a wheel with his sprag and save Owen from dumping a speeding train.

At the lunch whistle, Owen pulled a train of empty carts onto a rail siding. He tied a feed bucket of oats over the head of each mule, and climbed up onto the lead cart. His lamp lit only to about ten feet ahead. Glistening seepage water dripped steadily from the roof, the shadowy timber props and roof beams groaned a little, and an occasional sharp pop sounded from the rock.

He'd learned from Kevin that so long as the rock pops stayed regular and slow there wasn't much need to worry. Not too much, anyway. He stopped chewing on his sandwich and listened to a rapid burst of popping—if the pops suddenly came faster, you needed to start worrying. Roof falls maimed as many men as were killed, and a miner's worst fear was getting maimed. Owen tilted his head to shine the mining lamp on the nearest rock joints in the roof. The mules made it hard to hear anything with all their munching and crunching. A loud bang rattled the side of the cart next to his leg, and he nearly dropped his sandwich. He looked down to see the whippet standing beside him.

"You're one of the new boys, are you?" the sprag boy said. More like a mumble. Swatches of straight, black hair stuck out from under his cap. In the beam of lamplight his face shone clean from splashing through water all morning, and he looked a bit younger than Owen.

"I am. I've been in the breaker for a couple of years before, though," Owen said.

"I graduated to sprag boy from the breaker almost three years ago," the boy said. "Bit of a wonder how you moved right into a mule driver job without going through door boy or sprag boy. And you're Irish, too, aren't you?"

Owen raised his brow. Cheeky devil, this one was. "Right. Do you suppose they made a mistake?"

"Probably—though I've seen worse drivers. Are you a Catholic, too, then?"

"That too," Owen said.

"Why would you be telling your sins to a priest? Are you not allowed to go directly to God?"

The kid was a regular theologian. "I have so many of them it would take up too much of God's time," Owen said. "Are you Welsh, then?"

"I am. My name's Ian. And if I'm not a miner by the time I'm eighteen, you'll know I've died and gone to heaven."

Owen smiled. Something likeable about him, even if he was Welsh. "Right. Save a place for me, if so," Owen said.

"You can't get in. You're a popish Irish Catholic. Ta," he said, rapping the cart again and turning to go.

"My name's Owen."

"I know," Ian said.

CHAPTER EIGHTEEN—Soldier Brothers

The next couple of day's work went well for Owen. He envied Deak working inside a mining chamber, learning the methods and habits of a top miner like Martin. But roaming about had a few good points, too. He noticed which miners were most efficient, able to shoot down the face and leave work early, and observed what else went on in their chambers. He knew certain things to look for, too, thanks to Kevin. The miners' assistants didn't like Owen coming up to the coal face and nosing about, but he'd find an excuse to be there. He noticed some assistants were careless about moving the brattice canvases up closer to the face, to help deflect ventilation air forward to clear the fumes from blasting. Taking care of dull, routine jobs gave Owen his chance to look around.

A miner generally planned a drill hole layout to suit the checkerboard of joint spacing in the coal, and judging by the way the coal had broken up in previous blasts. He and his assistant used a couple of geared, hand-cranked breast drills that you leaned against with your chest to sink blasting holes in the face. They worked together to tamp black powder and fuse cord into the back of the blast hole, and plugged the front with clay stemming. Most of the miners tried to be ready to shoot a face by noon. After that blast the miner went home, but it took his assistants the rest of the day to move the broken coal back from the face and load the carts. There, Owen and his mules took over.

That was the thing that appealed to Owen: being in charge of your own work and planning out each day as a miner would. Maybe he didn't have a lot of experience yet, but he knew how to organize facts and think things through. He wasn't that careful about everything he did, but he'd always learned new things easily. Mining needed that logical turn of mind. You were faced with problems: how to blast down a certain face with the least amount of holes and powder. Is the roof rock safe here, or do we need a few more timber supports? You used your head to read the signs around you, and then you sorted out the best way to go about things.

On Saturday Owen and his da left the mine together. They stopped at the AOH lodge and went in. Owen felt good to be stopping there after work, though he wasn't a member yet. They took a small table in the back, near the meeting room. Mine workers kept stopping by their table and nodding Liam toward the meeting room. He waved them on and kept talking with Owen. Liam was in a dark mood and scowled when a couple of drunken miners stopped by on their way to the meeting. He wouldn't talk with any drunks and so they went on in.

"Got my first pay as a mule driver, though it wasn't as much of an increase from the breaker as I thought it would be," Owen said, wiping the foam from his mouth.

Liam shook his head. "They say the price per ton in Philadelphia went down this week, so they've cut pay scale for everyone again. Except, I'm sure, for the important people with the railroad. That's how things will always be without a labor union to represent us. I expect we'll all be back in debt by the end of the month."

"Won't my promotion and pay raise make any difference, then?" Owen said.

"It will, and your mother and I have been proud of the way you put it on the table each week. But we'll want to set a little of your earnings aside, to keep for you, so you'll have a stake when you're ready to go out on your own."

Owen tightened his clasped hands on the table. Now was as good a time as any to speak about it, "Mom isn't very happy, is she?"

Liam blinked. He lowered his eyes and moved his glass in small circles on the tabletop. "It's a hard life at times."

"But is everything going to be all right—with you and Mom?"

Liam stopped fidgeting with the glass and looked a little uncertainly at him. Gradually his face relaxed and he shook his head almost in a shudder. "Your mom and I, is it? I don't know. Somewhere things got away from me, I think, starting back when I sent your brothers off together in the war. After they were lost, it all but finished your mother and me. I expect the years since haven't been too easy on you, either, though she does love you. She just won't show it the way she once did with the others."

"You mean, like she once did with Sean?"

The corner of Liam's mouth twitched through a smile to a sort of sadness. "We don't mention him anymore, but he's still around. Yes, especially Sean. He was her favorite." Owen grew fearful that he might be close to tears and he tightened his clasped hands till they hurt. Liam went on, "I don't know if she'll ever be as open with her feelings again. I'd hoped that time would heal things, but it hasn't—not yet. There's little I know to do about it, either, only to go on doing the best I can. Before too long you'll be a grown man and on your own, then I'll wish I'd been a little closer with you. It's hard. Maybe I should walk away from the mineworker's fight, but I can't."

A man stopped by their table holding a hat. "We're taking up a collection to send the Widow Coyle's orphans to live with their grandparents back in Donegal," he said.

Liam dug into his pocket and tossed some money into the hat. Owen took out a coin and tossed that in, too. Some shouts and the sound of scuffling came from the meeting room. "I'd better go back there, now," Liam said, and downed his beer. "Sometimes no matter how just you think your goals are in a struggle, you might discover a few of your mates acting no different than—who was it in that newspaper—the Thugs of India? Yes, they couldn't be any worse than the man who robbed the mine boss at Shamokin after the assassination. A terrible shame to call down on the Mollies. Tell your mother I won't be home till late."

CHAPTER NINETEEN — Spies

The soda shop was packed by the time Owen arrived that evening. He spotted the boys and continued looking until he saw Maura at a girls' table. He went up to her, gestured back toward the boy's booth, and she got up and went with him.

"Would you look at this, the mule driver and herself come to join their former breaker mates," Peter said. "Isn't this a great democracy we're in, boys?"

Maura leaned on his shoulder and pushed him and Patrick over to make room on the bench. Owen sat across the table from them, beside Thomas.

Peter asked, "Did our newly promoted underground worker take a hit in his pay, too?"

"Aye, afraid so," Owen said. He ordered sarsaparillas for Maura and himself from the waiting girl, and told her to put everything on Peter's bill. She humphed, rolled her eyes, and hurried off. "Did any of you get a chance to see the Schuykill Journal?" Owen said.

"No, the delivery boy must have missed our shanty," Peter said. "So, what did it say?"

"This week makes the eighth and ninth killings by the Molly Maguires since the labor troubles began, and that maybe it's high time to start hanging a few Mollies. It said Jim Tully would make a good start, and if the official justice system couldn't get it done, the citizenry might be able to catch up the job for them."

"A fine, thoughtful paper, our Journal," Peter said. "Did they have any helpful suggestions for getting the people who shot Mrs. Coyle?"

"No, but I've some ideas on that," Owen said.

"Oh, no," Maura said. "Trouble."

Owen said, "It's not right that the paper didn't even call out the people who killed the widow. Those vigilantes made a couple of kids orphans, and the mine workers are having to take up collections to send them back to live with their grandparents."

"Probably not many people know who the vigilantes are," Thomas said.

"The butcher was one of them," Owen said. "I heard it from my da.

The vigilantes were masked, but the old fellow who works at the livery stable and rents a room at the Coyle house? He spotted the butcher's horse and caught out his voice."

Peter nodded and stared at him. "So what do we do?"

The girl came back with the sodas and Owen dug out some coins to pay her. She put the coins in her apron, leisurely mopped a few licks at the table with a rag, and stayed idling there. Maura blew a breath, slapped the tabletop, and glowered at her. The girl left quickly.

"Well?" Peter said.

"We could paint a sign on his window some night: vigilante shop— widow's assassin in here," Owen said.

They all gaped. Peter frowned and said, "Think the Pinkertons could find us out and send us all to jail?"

"We ought to do something, right? He was one of them," Owen said.

"But you don't really know," Maura sputtered. "Maybe the old fellow was mistaken—he looks like he's almost a hundred, and maybe he doesn't see or hear all that good."

"Sure, we don't really know," Patrick said, wide-eyed and rubbing at his cheek.

"Well, we could look into it," Owen said. "The old man also recognized another horse that's boarded at the stable, one belonging to a newcomer in town. He's said to be a bookkeeper at the railroad office, but a few mineworkers think he's a Pinkerton detective working alongside the railroad police. So, here's the plan: we do a bit of spying on the butcher and find out how tight the two of them are. We might even hear them talking about being in on the raid, and maybe our man will drop something about being a Pinkerton. Think how a sign in that window might look then: Butcher and Pinkertons ride with vigilantes who killed the widow."

Peter and Patrick turned to look at Maura. She went wide-eyed and had to clear her throat before she could speak, "But, well, we're not going to do anything at all unless we're absolutely sure about them being involved, right?"

"Absolutely," Owen said.

They walked over to the butcher shop afterward. The moon hadn't risen yet and the streets were dark and empty, except near the two saloons they passed. The shop was in the next block, and they turned into a delivery alley running behind the row of stores and living quarters, counting gateways as they passed. The butcher's gate was unlocked and they crept into the back yard. The buildings were two-story, with living quarters arranged above and behind the shops fronting on the street. A long rectangle of light fell across the yard from a ground-floor window. They stole around the edges of a garden area and pressed their backs to the wall near the lighted window. A narrow sliding-screen was set in the window opening beneath a raised sash, and they listened a few minutes to snatches of conversation and the bursts of laughter within. Owen turned slowly with his shoulder against the wall and stretched until he could just peer above the screen.

The butcher, the wagon shop owner, and another man sat at a table. Could be the detective there. Somewhere in his thirties, shaggy-haired, moustache, waistcoat. They were playing cards and drinking. When the stranger glanced up from his cards Owen quickly twisted away and flattened against the wall.

The next few seconds dragged by like an eternity. Then laughter and groans followed a loud thump on the table. Owen breathed again and motioned for Peter at the other side of the window to have a look. After Peter and the others had a turn, Owen changed places with Maura and she had a quick look. Seconds later chairs slid back and people moved about. Outside, they hunched over and ran through the yard, out the gate, and down the alley. They didn't stop running till they were in Thomas' back yard, behind his father's saloon. They sat at an outdoor table while Thomas slipped inside and came back with a small pail of beer.

"Everyone must be over to the AOH lodge tonight," he said. "It's near empty in our place. Da was talking with someone so I was able to pull this."

They passed it around and everyone took a turn, except Maura. Peter was having her on about it when she shut him up with a blistering stare. Maura wasn't able to hold down any alcoholic drink, and she'd brook no gaff about it, either.

"Well, we spotted an interesting stranger there visiting the butcher," Peter said. "We don't know if he's our man yet, but maybe we'll find that out soon enough."

Patrick said, "I don't know anything about him being a detective, but he does keep a horse at the stables. I've managed to catch a few Sunday afternoons of work there and I've groomed his horse."

"That part of it fits, then," Owen said. "Now maybe we could find the boarding house he stays at, and which room. Then if we spot him at a saloon we could maybe check his place for an unlocked door, or a window left open. We might be able to slip in and take a quick look for a badge, or something."

Maura slapped her leg, "We can't do that," she said. "If they caught any of us in his room they'd throw us in jail for sure."

Patrick said, "Okay, look, if he drops his horse off again while I'm working at the livery maybe I could clean and oil his saddlebags and have a quick look inside."

Maura said, "Not quite as bad, but I guess spying needs some risk. Okay, I was planning to look for a cleaning job in town on Monday. I could try the railroad office first, and maybe I'd be able to learn if our man really does work in there."

"Okay, that's the stuff," Owen said, "We'll give it a day or two and then make another night visit to listen in at the butcher's place."

CHAPTER TWENTY—Church Outcasts

Fr. Morrison read the bishop's excommunication of the Mollies at Mass on Sunday. Owen's face went white. It was every bit like getting hit with a punch to the stomach. He turned to look at his da's face. Liam's brow hunkered down and his jaw muscles twitched. Fr. Morrison went on, jabbing a finger in the air as if to point out the secret oath-takers, railing on about the continued violence, certainly it's the evil work of the Mollies, and the reason for the bishop issuing his edict. The Mollies were cast out from the Church and would be denied the sacraments and salvation. If a man was known to be a Molly, his friends, even his own family, were to shun him. Pray for his soul, yes, but have no more to do with him. He's been cut off from the Church.

Owen could hardly breathe, and then Liam stood up. He bumped past people sitting in the pew and Owen jumped up to follow after him. The church fell silent as they hurried up the aisle. Another man got to his feet in one of the rows to the rear, then another, and Liam and Owen were out the door. They walked at a furious pace down the hillside and never spoke a word. Turning away from the main road they walked a mile out to the abandoned Monroe Mine, a place Owen had often been with his friends.

A long, slab-like heap of a culm pile stretched a quarter-mile along the hillside. They walked along the old track bed on top of the pile. The rails and crossties had been taken up long ago, to be of use elsewhere. A light wind came up and black dust devils spiraled up and danced along the culm pile. They stopped and Liam folded his arms across his chest and turned one way, then another, shaking his head, murmuring, and staring out from the dark mountain of waste. Below, large pieces of dumped slate had slid down the culm slope and entered a creek flowing along the toe. The sounds of water sloshing and rippling through the slate carried up to them.

Owen had to know for sure. "So then, da, you are a Molly Maguire?"

Liam swept back fingers through his hair and took a deep breath. "I've admitted nothing walking out on that ranting, and I told you before, don't ask about things dangerous for you to know. Think of it, now—you could be questioned in future."

Owen tipped a tall slab of rock with his foot and it slid and tumbled like a drunk pitching down the slope. "I'm not going to listen to what Fr. Morrison says, da, and I'm not attending Mass anymore."

"Hold your tongue, you're not to stay away from church. You're not yet able to understand and decide on any life and death issues for yourself," Liam said.

"But look what they've done; how can they themselves deny salvation to anyone—isn't it up to God?"

"There's nothing left but for the Mollies to find out, isn't it? Any Molly might not like what the priest said, but the Church has been around a long time and might have gotten a few things right over the time. God help us all."

"They don't care about the right or wrong of a mineworker's fight. Being a man and trying to follow your own conscience may be a right," Owen said.

"Are we now hearing from a doctor of the Church, then?" Liam said. "It cannot be known for certain what a Molly does for justice will not condemn him before God. A Molly can only pray it will be so."

"But if I go to church and you stay away it'll be like they've thrown you out and I'm accepting it. That's just what they want."

Liam grasped Owen's shoulders and waited till Owen looked into his face. "You'll be going to church because until you're old enough and on your own, I'm telling you to go. And you'll also go to your religion classes at the confraternity. Are we together on that?"

Owen would rather have chewed the sole off his shoe, but he had to agree. He kept shaking his head till he could find his voice. "Yes, I'll do as you say," he said.

Liam didn't come home for dinner that evening. The day had been warm and still and the shanty was stuffy, so Owen ate outside. The air shimmered above the scruffy, tree-studded hills to the north. A dark blotch in the top of a spindly tree gave some shrill cries and lifted upward, its wing beats jerky at first, and then it settled into effortless glides just above the treetops. A glint of sunlight marked it as a Red Tail Hawk.

"How was it on the mountaintop today?" Owen asked his mother.

She stopped stirring the tallow and ash soap heating over the fire and glanced toward him, then resumed stirring. "Peaceful," she said. "It's a holy place, quiet."

Owen said, "It wasn't too peaceful and quiet today at another holy place. Fr. Morrison told us the bishop has excommunicated the Mollies. Da got up and left in the middle of the sermon and I went with him."

Aine laid aside her spatula and brushed loose strands of hair from her face. She was quiet for a few moments. "Will you not be going back to church again?"

"I don't want to, but da said I had to go. I was wondering if sometimes after church I might join you on your mountain. At least some Sundays, and just for a little while, maybe an hour or so."

She stood up, started to say something, but turned to look toward the lowering sun. Shadows had started creeping across the valleys and up the western flanks of the hills. The hawk shrieked again in the stillness, but was nowhere to be seen. "Leave me be, Owen," she said. She picked up a pail and hurried off toward the water spigot.

CHAPTER TWENTY-ONE—Work Mates

Owen rode the cage down with Ian on Monday morning. About twenty workers jammed in together, no one talking much, only a few words back and forth. An occasional spurt of tobacco juice spattered onto the timbered shaft wall as the cage lowered. The air smelled of stale body odor and old socks. The ride was jerky, the cage often dropping quickly a few inches before banging up short again as the cable spooled out. The air became heavier and more humid as the cage went deeper. Shadows flew in and out as light from the miner's lamps danced past big, square-set timbers in the wall holding back the earth. Minutes later the cage jarred to a stop, the door banged open, and men called to each other as they strode out to their work places.

"I'll need to stop in on my da for a second," Owen said, breaking off from Ian.

"Will I wait for you, then?" Ian said.

"Suit yourself."

Owen went through the brattice door and into the airway tunnel.

Liam had finished charging the furnace and was sitting on a stool, watching the fire roar. He turned and lifted his thumb in salute when he noticed his son.

Owen set down the lunch pail. "Mom sent this. You weren't able to make it home again, so," he said, bunching his hands in the hem of his pullover.

Liam nodded and glanced about before speaking. "I stayed to an all-night meeting that went nowhere. The newspaper has Tully's trial moved up to Wednesday, and there's to be more arrest warrants out later this week. The Coal and Iron Police are building up to make the arrests."

"Are you scared, da?"

The corner of Liam's mouth twitched as he stared into the fire. His cap was off, hair disheveled, and he needed a shave. "I'm thinking a life without justice is no life at all," he said.

He got up, tugged his cap on, and began shoveling coal to the furnace. Owen stood watching, not knowing what to do or say. If his da wasn't scared, Owen sure was. He went back through the brattice door and found Ian waiting for him. They started down the gangway with the last group of workers coming from the lift.

Owen said, "Why'd you wait to walk with me—what'll your Welsh buddies think?"

Ian shrugged. "Who cares? What I want to know is why you've got all those statues with bleeding hands, and bleeding hearts, and those tormented, miserable crucifixes?"

Owen turned to look at him, "What in—" and almost stumbled across a mound of fallen rock, just managing to catch his balance and go on. They continued so as Owen darted looks at him. His theologian buddy was at it again. Owen said, "Maybe they're supposed to help put you in a prayerful way of mind. Anything wrong with that?"

"Do you have a crucifix over your bed?"

Owen hesitated, to see if he was serious or just taunting him. Ian only plodded along, watching his steps along the steel tracks. "Well, no, but we used to have a Sacred Heart picture on a wall, and a statue of the Infant of Prague on a windowsill—that's Jesus; don't bother asking me to explain. My mother put both of them away after my two brothers were killed in the war with the South."

"Have you stopped praying then?"

"Well, I still give it a go now and then. Do you pray?"

"Of course."

They were at the stable and hesitated before going their separate ways.

"Will I help on some of your supply runs later this morning, then?" Ian asked.

Owen thought it over. During the first couple of hours the mule drivers took out any standing coal carts from the previous day, and then there were the supply and maintenance runs till the new faces were shot down. There'd be a little time in the morning when Ian wouldn't have to worry about runaway loaded carts. Ian made for an odd sidekick, but what of it? "Okay, I'll pick you up on one of my supply runs," Owen said. Ian gave a thumbs-up before hurrying down the tracks to his station.

Later in the morning Owen picked him up and they rode back to one of the newly opened chambers deep in the mine. The miner there had been hired on wages, a new arrangement, since miners had always before worked on independent contracts. Now, the railroad wanted better control of costs, but the new arrangement made a miner just another wage employee. That was dispiriting to

Owen. If the owners got away with it, the pride of someday becoming a skilled, independent miner would be diminished to him.

At the chamber they offloaded a can of powder, fuse cord, tamping stick, stemming clay, timbers, wedging shims, and wood lagging. They carried in the blasting supplies first. The miner was an old Welshman named Erwin, and glad to have the work, even on wages. He pointed to where he wanted the supplies, watched them unload it, and said little. Ian knew the miner's assistant, William, but didn't speak with him. After they had carried in the last of the timber, William came over.

"Ian, you and your man here scale down some of the loose roof rock before you leave. My miner wants to shoot early, and I'll need to stay at the face to help him load."

Owen and Ian exchanged glances. It was risky work, Owen knew that from Kevin's stories, and he knew it was something William was supposed to do himself. He said to Ian, "We might help them for a while, but then I'd have to get back to my hauling work."

William looked at him, spit on the floor, and regarded him again. He took Ian by the shoulder and led him away, with Owen following. They walked to several places where William pointed up to shadowy lines in the smooth, slate roof—places where clay-filled joints had allowed a slab to loosen and to slip a little below an adjacent one. Water dripped from some of these joints, lubricating a continued, slow slippage. The mining practice was to pry them down before they fell on a worker, unexpectedly.

William brought over a couple of long iron rods flattened to a tongue at one end. The boys took them to one of the loose slabs and started prying at the joints from opposite sides. It was hard work levering the heavy steel bar overhead, and neck and shoulder muscles became knotted and ached. After a few minutes of prying, the huge rock slab they worked on shuddered suddenly, and dropped between them with a thunderous clap. Owen frantically swiped mud splatter from his eyes to look for Ian. The beam of Owen's mining lamp glinted back at him from Ian's widened eyes.

"Lord Almighty, we were almost called home on that one," Ian said.

CHAPTER TWENTY-TWO—Blasting Hazards

They scaled down a few more slabs before Owen got worried about the time. Erwin had started laying out his fuses and William followed behind, tamping clay stemming into the blasting holes. They'd be ready to shoot soon. Just then the ground jumped with a dull bumping noise. A miner somewhere farther along the airway had already blasted down a coalface.

Owen grabbed Ian's arm; "We'd better go. They're already shooting and it's time to start moving the coal."

Ian seemed impressed with having been assigned the risky business of scaling down rock and hated to quit, but he knew they had to get on with their own jobs. They picked up a train of loaded carts at a nearby chamber and headed back to the shaft. Another train of carts loaded with today's coal was waiting ahead of them as they got near Slick Grade, and Ian jumped off to cover his post. Owen held back his mules till Ian had the driver ahead of them safely over the grade, then he started through himself. Sarah and Elsie were fresh and held back the carts well enough, so that Ian had only to jog alongside as Owen rolled through.

As lunchtime drew near Owen made another run back into the mine with a train of empty carts. Ian sat on an empty powder keg at the far end of his station. No loaded trains were in sight and Owen waved him alongside.

"It's lunch break; let's see how Erwin did with his blasting," he said. "We'll eat on the way in, and you can get back here on the run before the break is over."

Ian went for his lunch pail and caught up to the cart. He leapt on board and they made short work of sandwiches and jars of tea along the way, stopping only to uncouple carts at two of the crosscut tunnels. They passed another driver holed up for lunch in a crosscut. The kid craned his neck to see them in the dim light, and he exchanged greetings with Ian. Owen called out a hello, too, but the driver wouldn't respond. A Welsh kid—he'd probably rather choke.

They took their last two carts through a crosscut to Erwin's mining chamber. While the boys were uncoupling the mules from the empty carts, Erwin and William came hurrying back from the face.

"Fire in the Hole," called Erwin as they darted behind the carts and crouched.

The blast warning—Owen grabbed the reins of his mules and turned them about. They were startled and acted up, but Ian jumped in to grab Elsie's bit. They'd no sooner hurried the mules in behind the carts than a crumpling whoosh of air blew past them. A few small rocks clattered off the crosscut ribs. The mules straightened their long ears up and shied back, but then were quiet. They'd been around blasting before. Owen hadn't ever been so close to a face blast, and his heart pounded. They went back into the chamber and it was hard to see with the black dust swirling about.

"Use your jackets lads and clear this air so we can get back to work," called Erwin, after they'd reentered the chamber.

He and William fanned the sooty air with their jackets to force it out toward the chamber entry. The boys removed their jackets and joined in. The air hardly moved and eye-watering gases stayed heavy near the coalface. Owen noticed the brattice curtain needed to shunt ventilating air toward the coalface had been blown over by the blast, and he got Ian to help him right it. That helped, and in a few minutes the gases and fumes cleared enough to see more clearly. Erwin came to join them behind the brattice, and catch his breath. He coughed and hawked-up a few black gobs.

He said to William, "Take a look along the face and see if there's been any misfires."

William said, "Come up with me, Ian, and see about a miner's work."

Ian hesitated. "Dangerous stuff, be careful," Owen whispered to him. He'd heard enough to know that getting blown up by slow-burning misfires probably ranked right up with rock-falls and gas explosions. He'd seen the hollow-eyed men hopping about on crutches in town, or waving their blunt-ended arms. But what would you look for? A bright new length of fuse cord still smoldering?

William led the way, looking closely at some places along the blasted face, and hurrying Ian to keep pace with him. The shattered coal had slumped and spread out over the floor beneath them. Halfway across the mounded coal William stopped and raised a hand. He leaned forward to look at the standing face, and backed away. Erwin got to his feet as they came hurrying back.

"Couldn't tell if the fuse was cut or it'd misfired near the far end of the face," William said.

Erwin turned and spat. "Bloody bother. We're already late with our loads. Might just be a good business I'm on wages instead of contract. We'll give her another ten minutes to see what she'll do. You, boy," he said to Owen, "Grab a pail near the entry and scoop up some water from the gutter. We might just try to douse her and pull the fuse clear if she doesn't blow first."

Owen looked from Erwin to the dark, jagged face of coal. "You mean you want me to walk out there right now?"

"No—next Sunday," he said, and gave him a hard shove out.

Owen stumbled from behind the brattice and ran for the chamber entry. He slowed down only after he'd made it outside to the airway tunnel. After filling a pail from the gutter, he stood quietly to think about it. If the charge didn't go off, he might be the paddy they'd send forward to douse the fuse and pull it clear, and it wasn't even his job. He decided to delay a bit more—had to be almost another five minutes—when suddenly an explosion ripped through the air.

He dropped the bucket and flattened his back against a timber prop. A few big rocks pitched out from the chamber and a hail of rock chips behind them, not as big a blast as before, but enough to rip apart someone reaching for a fuse. He went to the entry and looked in; Erwin and William walked to the face and Ian trailed after them. Owen shouted for Ian to come out, grabbed the mules, and was already headed toward the gangway when Ian came running. Lunch break was over and they hurried away to their own jobs.

CHAPTER TWENTY-THREE—The Detective

On confraternity night a remembrance service was held for Tim in the church meeting room. The youths waited in line to light votive candles set along the edge of the stage, and some lingered to say a silent prayer. In the stark world of the coal patch, death was a frequent visitor but Tim's terrible passing had been especially wrenching to many of the young people.

Later, Owen listened dutifully to Fr. Morrison's spiritual farewell to Tim, and to the assurances of his happiness in heaven. Owen wanted to feel there was nothing to fear about dying. Just so long as it happened quickly. It was hard to think of anything very promising in the sermons about a hereafter: the Beatific Vision— seeing God, the house with many rooms—all those coded catechism hints. Vague stuff that only saints might get a grip on.

After class discussions, when the youths were moving chairs back to clear the floor for dancing, Fr. Morrison came over to talk with Owen. They went outside and Owen waited while Fr. Morrison tamped his pipe full of tobacco.

"You gave me a bit of a start when you walked out on my sermon last Sunday," he said, after drawing on his pipe and releasing a pungent cloud of smoke.

"My da left, so I had to go."

"Has he let you know he's a Molly?"

Owen pulled a piece of sedge from the side of the path and twisted it into a half-hitch. "I know he believes in what the Mollies are fighting for—like taking up for workingmen."

"And killing other men?"

His hard look withered Owen. In a storybook sort of way Owen could cheer for the Mollies, but he couldn't say killing anyone was right. Even if it was for labor justice. He said, "It's hard to see how that part is right, but I hope it's something God might forgive them."

"Even after the Church has warned them, commanded them to turn away from their unholy rebellion against faith and society, and now has cast them out from our corpus of believers?"

Owen looked past him. It wasn't right to argue with a priest; still, he couldn't abandon his da either. Maura had come to the doorway and looked out at them. Owen's throat was stitched tight, but he got it out anyway. "You taught us that if you told God you were sorry for your sins before you died, you were always forgiven. Is it not true for the Mollies, too—even now?"

Fr. Morrison puffed smoke furiously and his face tightened. After a time his posture eased and he said, "I hope no one presumes too heavily on an imperfect contrition and God's mercy at some last hour." He took a few more draws on his pipe. "I'm glad you came tonight, Owen. I was afraid you might stay away altogether after last Sunday." He knocked the pipe out against an uplifted heel, nodded, and went off toward the rectory.

Owen stepped inside the doorway and joined Maura. Patrick was leaning against a wall watching the dancing, and Owen nodded to him. He caught the attention of Peter and Thomas on the dance floor and signaled to them, also. They went outside and walked to the front of the church to sit on the concrete steps. In the darkness, patches of lighted windows and domes of light above the saloons gave shape to the town spread out below.

"Report time," Owen said. "Did you find out anything, Patrick?"

"I got a quick look at a packet of letters our man had in his saddlebag. One was a Pinkerton Detectives' envelope addressed to a Jonas Sherman, and two others were from the railroad to the same person. That doesn't jibe with the name he uses at the livery, though. He's on the roster as Buell Gallagher."

Maura said, "Yes, that's the name on his office door in the railroad building, too. I saw him working in there. I didn't get a job in the building; they already had a cleaning girl. Anyhow, I saw him again today when I helped my father to the courthouse for the start of Tully's trial. Our man Gallagher spoke with the railroad lawyers quite a bit."

Owen nodded. "He's a railroad detective for sure. Did they have any witnesses speak today at the trial?"

Maura said, "They were only just putting together their jury—looked like they were all German farmers from over in west county. A few told the judge they couldn't speak much English, but that didn't seem to count for anything. They all went into the jury box."

"Poor Tully," Owen said. "I hope he gets a few Dutchmen that know the language and care about a fair trial. Well, we need to do whatever we can. I think we're closer to connecting the vigilantes raid with the railroad detective and the butcher. Maura and I can go over to the butcher's house tonight and do a little more investigating. Peter, you take a look over there tomorrow night, and Thomas, you're on for the next night. That suit everyone?"

Maura and Owen stayed off the main street and entered the alleyway from another street over. A crazed dog barked and clawed a fence gate as they hurried past. Farther on, they slipped through the gateway into the butcher's yard and crept up to the lighted window. Owen flattened his back against the wall and looked past the corner of the window casing. The butcher was at the table in an undershirt, reading a newspaper by lamplight. Owen turned away and slid down to sit on the ground. Maura slid down beside him.

"Nothing happening—he's alone," Owen whispered. "But we'll wait a bit and make a proper job of it. Let's give the moon enough time to clear the church steeple."

Dogs barked in the distance. Loud, arguing voices rose from the next street over—maybe from outside the saloon. A sharp crackle of firearms split the air. The arguing went on as before, so probably they hadn't successfully murdered each other. Moths dropped from the lighted window and fluttered about them. Maura slipped her hand into Owen's and he flinched. He turned to her, squeezed her hand, and looked again to the church steeple. Better stay focused on spying. A few seconds later, footsteps and voices sounded in the alley. They stiffened—whoever it was had stopped at the back gate. Maura and Owen backed away from the window and into the darker shadows along the side fence. Two men entered the yard and came up the walkway, stopping as one of them lifted a bottle to drink. They went on to the porch door and knocked.

"Why have we to involve the creepin' butcher in this?" the man with the bottle slurred.

"He's head of the Citizen's Committee," the other man said. "We want to enlist their support for what needs to be done. Look smart now, Kegan, he's coming."

The door opened and light shone on the dapper dressed man standing at the stairs. Buell Gallagher, or Jonas Sherman, whoever. The other man wore rough-cut work clothes. The butcher stepped back from the doorway and invited them in. Buell waited till Kegan stumbled past, then went in after him. Maura and Owen crept back to the window as the men settled themselves at the table.

Buell introduced Crimp Kegan as a mine worker, arrested as a suspected accomplice in the Tully case, but who had agreed to be a prosecution witness. He was now ready to help the beleaguered citizens of the town dispatch the murderous Molly Maguires. The butcher had great praise for all that, and Crimp joined in with a few of his own choice curses on the Mollies.

Time passed with much clinking of glasses and aimless stories, and Crimp began talking of his experiences as a Molly. Buell kept him focused on that, pulling him back when he wandered from any exploits not connected with the Mollies. Buell then coaxed him to tell the story of how he had accompanied Jim Tully to the boardinghouse of the two blacklegs, and how Tully had shot dead the Welshman in the gunfight that followed. Crimp also admitted to wounding the Cornishman who'd managed to flee. No matter about those past errors, Buell told him. He'd been coerced by the Mollies, but he'd finally faced up to their depravity and evil ways.

"And you're the man who can bring them down now, when you testify in court," Buell said.

"Ahhh," the butcher crooned, "Of course, you were in on all the planning and could testify firsthand as they say. You'll have all the names, naturally."

There was a long pause. "It's Tully on trial, isn't it?" Crimp said. "What need is there to talk of other Mollies?"

"Everyone who's a member of that murderous organization is just as guilty as Tully," Buell said. "The quickest way to stop their savagery is to have an exemplary hanging of as many of them as possible. In another week or two we should have hanging cases ready against a couple of dozen more Mollies."

"We only talked of testimony against Tully," Crimp said.

Buell sighed. "Suit yourself," he said. "You can hang with Tully as an accomplice to murder, or you can give up the rest of those criminals and go free. We were prepared to stake you to a new beginning somewhere."

More drink was poured, glasses whacked against the table, and the silence stretched out. "We need the names of the Mollies known to you," Buell said. "I'll take notes. You'll be appearing as a witness for the prosecution tomorrow, and some of our Mollies may try to flee the region when they learn of your collaboration. It's best we're prepared, so it'll be the job of our Citizen's Committee to keep watch on our suspects until we're ready to arrest them."

Another round of drinks was downed and Crimp gasped as his glass hit the table. He started giving names. Owen looked beside him at Maura. She leaned into the patch of light coming down from the window and wrote in a pad as Crimp called out the names. Liam Dougherty was one of the names.

CHAPTER TWENTY-FOUR—The Mollies List

Owen lay on his bed in trousers and undershirt, listening to the sawing of crickets outside. The window was propped full open to catch any drift of a breeze, but the night air was still. The green smell of leafing trees replaced the winter's sour smell of wet culm piles. Owen flopped an arm across his forehead. Probably shouldn't stay here another week. The list was only the names of people Crimp identified as Mollies, but maybe they just wanted to hang all of them whether they were guilty of shooting someone or not. He groaned and flopped over onto his stomach again.

Maybe his da and some of the others were really against the assassinations, and wanted to do things differently—but they were outvoted. Yes, but even so, they might be convicted, regardless. He wondered where they could go. They had the cousins up in New York, where his brothers stayed when they went up to enlist. They could go up there, and his da and he could get factory jobs. Probably like being in jail, standing in one place all day, year in and year out, doing the same thing, always the same thing. He'd feel like a failure if he didn't become a miner—but there was just no choice about it.

He fell asleep before da came home, and woke when the front door creaked open. He jumped up, pulled on his boots, and caught Liam before he got to his bedroom door.

"What's this?" Liam said as Owen handed him the slip of paper.

"It's a list of Mollies they got from an informer." Owen told him about spying at the butcher's house.

Liam sat at the table, lit the lamp, and stared at the paper a few seconds. Owen took the chair across from him. Liam pushed the slip of paper toward him, "Read it off," he said. "Softly, now, so it doesn't disturb your mother."

He read off the names. Liam nodded at some, scoffed at others. Owen had to stop after Liam's name, but then he managed to go on. After finishing he asked, "What'll we do—maybe get away, go to New York?"

Liam clasped his hands on the table. "We'll stay and see what comes of it. Their informer, Crimp, is a newcomer to these hills, and his inclusion in the Tully affair was not sanctioned by most. He's a thief, the one who turned a Mollies' action into a common robbery.

He's had other serious problems with the law and the jury cannot believe much of what this man might say. I'll need to let the others know of this situation, and they can make their own decisions."

Owen ran his hand through his hair. It was just like the picture he'd seen of the Irish Brigade at Chancellorsville, plodding ahead with fixed bayonets while the Rebs mowed down their ranks with cannon fire. His da wasn't even being reasonable. The railroad had all the money, lawyers, and police you could ever imagine and wanted to get rid of every single Molly, guilty or not.

Liam got up from his chair. "God love you for wanting to rescue your da, but mind that you stay away from the butcher's house. If you were caught it might go badly with you, seeing as how they already suspect me." He waited till Owen nodded before going to his bedroom.

Owen stayed sitting. His hands trembled on the table, his fingers knotting together. He didn't want his da fighting against the law but he didn't know what he could do about it. He bit his lip and looked around the room. Moonlight splashed across the floor and ran up the far wall. A soft glow reflected from rows of dishes in the breakfront and off the polished, dark-stained wood of rocker chairs near the fireplace. Da must have liked the sort of boy he was, good at learning, confident of being a miner, but he never knew what his mom thought. Maybe she was only staying because she felt a duty to Owen—might that be all there was to it? The best sharing they did was sitting together outside, always him to do the talking, but seeing her eyes light up or catching her smile at some foolish thing he'd said. He wanted to be closer, but he'd take whatever they had.

But now, it all could end, and she'd go back to that faraway land. He'd never be able to forget her. He pushed himself up from the table and went to his room.

Over the rest of the week Owen and Ian managed to spend part of each morning together, helping and getting to know miners and their assistants. They were all Welsh, except one assistant, an Irishman, who'd been a miner in the north of England. Owen was frustrated to learn the man had been an assistant at the Hopmore mine for four years, and still hadn't gotten his own chamber. He thought of Ian's timetable—a miner by eighteen—that would be a bold stroke for an Irish lad, but now there were other, more serious problems.

On Saturday night the friends met in Kevin's shanty instead of their usual get-together in the soda shop. Things were uncomfortable in town now that the trial was on. Thomas arrived with a copy of a Philadelphia newspaper he'd picked up from his da's saloon, and the Tully trial was on page one. He offered it to Kevin, but he only waved it away and went out to look for his cat. Thomas read the front page to the boys, stumbling on the florid styling of the language, and at last handed the paper over to Owen. Owen took it and cautiously read aloud:

When the dark, inner workings of the Molly Maguires are revealed in these proceedings they will show a conspiracy such as the world has rarely met. These demons have satiated themselves on years of lawlessness, bloodshed, plunder, and anarchy. The anthracite region has been laid waste under their depredations. What God placed there for a bountiful harvest by a free people the Molly Maguire thugs have trampled into a quagmire of death and rapine. Property and capital have been held to ransom, honest labor throttled into submission, and the Mollies, drunk on the blood of their victims, dance their jigs over the violated figure of Justice, lying bleeding and supine. The roots of a great evil have been discovered, and must now be exterminated.

"Gripping," Peter said. "Sounds like there're thousands of Mollies riding horseback over the countryside, hacking down people with scythes and clubs."

"That tired old crone, Justice, was bleeding before the Mollies ever rode in," Thomas said.

Owen looked at Maura. "You're not saying anything. If they're writing stuff like this in the newspapers a Molly might be convicted by just showing up for trial."

Maura nodded and was quiet a few seconds. "They had Crimp in court today," she said. "He pointed out Tully as the one who shot and killed the blackleg. The railroad's lawyer demanded that Tully be hanged, and a lot of townspeople in the courtroom stood up and cheered. The whole jury looked scared. Tully's lawyers are to finish up on Monday, but the air of things seemed dead set against him. My da thinks they'll surely hang him."

Owen slapped the paper down. "Didn't Tully's lawyer make anything of Crimp being an informer to save himself? Maybe Tully wasn't even there and Crimp did all the shooting himself."

Maura said, "Crimp just shrugged off all the defense lawyer's questioning and kept repeating his own story. Owen, I'm afraid for your da if they arrest him with the other men on that list."

Kevin opened the front screen to shoo in the cat, and the door slapped shut again. Owen wound the newspaper into a tight roll and tapped it on the edge of his chair. "Maybe he's got some plan—I just don't know," he said. "Maybe he doesn't even care anymore." He got up from the chair, tossed the newspaper aside, and left.

CHAPTER TWENTY-FIVE—A Meeting Place

The following week the railroad decided to bring more coal under production and brought in new foremen and tunneling crews. The gangway and air tunnels needed to be dug deeper in. The workers normally left a wide pillar of coal standing between the gangway and airway tunnels, a necessity to support the overlying rock after the tunnels were dug out. On orders to save money, the bosses had ordered a narrower, twenty-foot wide pillar be used instead of the usual thirty-foot width, so that less coal would be left wasted in the pillar.

Monday morning Owen hauled in some mine props and tunnel roof beams needed for the operation. He decided to bring Ian back in with him at lunchtime, and they could listen to rock noises when the work stopped. He wanted to observe whether the thinner pillar made more rock pops, and compare it with what he'd been hearing alongside the wider pillar.

He picked Ian up a little before noon. They were dropping off empty carts at the next to last chamber when they heard the burst, almost like a fusillade of cannon fire, followed by thudding sounds of rock falling into the gangway. They quickly uncoupled the last of their carts and rode the mule team to the deep end of the gangway. When they got close to the falling rock it got difficult to see in the heavy cloud of black dust swirling out from the new tunneling. Owen forced his mules forward, until he could begin to make out what happened. The pillar had failed and the roof of both tunnels was collapsed farther in. In the distance men cried out, others rushed about with picks and shovels climbing over rubble, tearing away at rock piles.

"Bring your mules over here," a man shouted, as he struggled to pry a heavy rock slab off his mate.

The boys dismounted, unhooked the mules from the carts, and backed them in. The man grabbed the ends of their chain traces and looped them around the rock slab.

"Pull!" he yelled over the awful groaning of the man pinned under the rock.

Owen looked back, uncertain, but when the man waved him on he snapped the whip over the heads of Sarah and Elsie. Ian yanked at their bits, and the mules strained forward. The rock barely budged as the man kept the chain snug and urged them on. Owen cracked his whip again and the rock pulled ahead with a lurch. The trapped man let out a scream as the rock slid free. His mate tossed the chain aside and dragged the injured man to one side, then ran to help dig for others trapped beneath the debris. Men shouted and clawed and pushed rock slabs down from the pile as fast as they could pry them loose. The roof began crumbling again, and Owen ran up onto the pile to help men set a prop to the roof. Ian ran to get more help from the front of the mine.

Workers finally cleared the roof fall and carried out three injured men. A laborer, whose name Owen remembered being on the list of Mollies, passed word that a work stoppage would be held the next day to protest the unsafe working conditions. A few Welsh swore to join in.

Owen's arms and back ached when he sat alone to eat that evening—his da hadn't come home after work. Boiled potatoes and pig's knuckles, with peas from the garden. Meals had been getting frugal again with the company continuing to hack at wages. After eating Owen took his mug of tea outside and found Aine planting a new section of garden. It took a lot of work to level a flat strip of ground on the steep, rocky hillside. She had four terraces marching down the slope, each about twenty feet long and a few feet wide. He finished his tea and walked down the stone steps to join her on the new, bottom terrace.

"Here, let me help," he said. "What are you planting now?"

"Carrots—are you sure you want to help? You've been working all day."

"So have you. Give me some of those seeds and show me what you want."

She pointed to the thin row she'd scratched along the length of the terrace bed and showed him the seed spacing she was using. She left him kneeling with the dish of seeds while she went up the path to get another. Owen soon found the nimbleness of his fingers was not so good after having spent two years in the breaker picking shale. He had a terrible time sorting the tiny specks of seed and getting them an inch apart in the row. By the time Aine came back he had used almost all his seeds, and was only halfway down the row. She looked at the small amount left in his dish, and walked back along the row staring down at the clumps of seed he'd dribbled in along the way. She let out a groan.

"Not very good, is it?" he said, standing up from the row.

She shook her head. "That's all right. I'll get them thinned out. Go along with you now."

A tired look came over Owen—he set his plate down, reached over, and took her hand. She looked at him, startled. "Let's sit down and talk a minute, okay?" he said. She held back a moment, then followed his lead and sat beside him on the raised curbstones along the edge of the terrace. As if nervous she might bolt away he covered their clasped hands with his free hand. "I don't want you to go back and live with your sister in Ireland, mom. I want you to stay right here. I'd miss you too bad, and I'd be miserable." He frowned and put on his most serious look. "Anyhow, wouldn't you want to be around to see your own grandchild?"

She stared at him with widened eyes. "Has something happened— is it Maura, then?"

Owen's grip on her hand tightened. "No, no, it's not that, nothing has happened. I mean, that's a possibility. I mean, marrying—not the other. Well, no, that's not right, either—eventually a kid. Could be Maura, and a kid—but afterward."

Aine shook her head and blinked at his avalanche of words. She was relieved and eased her hand from his grip, clasped her knees, and looked out on the towering stacks of white clouds edging across the mountains from the east. High-flying tree swallows banked and swooped in the last rays of sunlight. She said, "What am I to do with you, Owen? We can't be tightening bonds now when it's almost time for you to go. You'll need to be far stronger to meet what's ahead of you in this life."

"Well, maybe that's true enough, but it'd be grand to have you around for the while, to see me handle it all."

He watched her. She sighed with exasperation, maybe even smiled—could have been that. This was real progress.

It felt odd to Owen not going to work on Wednesday. Liam said he'd be at a meeting of the mineworkers in town, to see whether a new labor union might be attempted. He didn't give it much chance for success.

The boys and Maura met early at Kevin's shanty and walked to the old Monroe Mine. The morning was warm and the wind gusty. Swirls of grit bit at their faces as they walked along the crest of the culm pile outside the mine. At the end of the culm the Monroe had a decline entry, a long, sloping tunnel that followed the coal seam as it dipped lower into the hillside. All the easy seams, like this, ones that could be mined starting right at ground surface, were the first to be worked. As the mining went deeper, the workers were carried down into the mine in an open, tracked cart. A winch shed for lowering and raising the cart had been built at the top of the decline. The door hung off its hinges and they lifted it open and went inside. A huge drum-reel, stripped of its cable, faced a hinged flap door in the front wall. Behind the reel stood a battered and rusted boiler. The steam engine had long since been removed. They sat on benches at a rough-hewn plank table at the rear of the shed. Daylight streamed through a shattered window in the rear wall. Thomas brought out playing cards and a pint bottle with a few inches left in it that he'd nipped from his da's saloon. Patrick took out a pouch of tobacco and reached up onto a shelf to take down a tin canister of torn newspaper squares and matches. He rolled cigarettes for them all.

"Cut them," Thomas said, pushing the shuffled deck to Owen and leaning to get a light from Peter.

Maura walked around the room, looking at the odds and ends of the machinery, pipes, and rusted pressure gages. It was the first time they'd taken her on a visit to the shed. "Did someone used to live here?" she asked. A canvas was spread on the floor in a narrow space on the far side of the boiler. A second roll of canvas and a lumpy, soiled pillow lay on top. A couple of wood shelves were nailed to the wall above the bedding.

"That stuff was there from when we first started using this place," Peter said. "Maybe it was someone that hid out from the draft during the war."

"Or maybe just another poor mine laborer that couldn't afford any other place to live," Maura said. "Left a lovely hand-carved crucifix hanging on the wall. We should keep a jar of holy water here, and fill the little dish on the crucifix whenever we're up here."

"What's lovely about a crucifix?" Owen said, studying the cards dealt him. "The church is forever wanting to keep everyone meek and humble with reminders of their sinful nature."

Maura came out from the boiler and stood behind him, looking at his cards. "I think signs like that are a comfort, sometimes," she said. "They don't have to be just about sin. I'm going outside to walk around a bit."

"Blessings, my child—don't fall down the slope. Two for me," Peter said, slapping his discards onto the table.

When it came to Owen's turn he was still staring at his cards without really seeing them. He used to talk with Maura about that sort of thing, back in seventh and eighth grade, when he started pulling back from all that piety. She wouldn't argue, but she was good as a sprag boy at slowing his cart down.

They played cards for the next half-hour without much talk. Patrick said he was on to sing at a wedding Mass for an uncle next week, and they were all invited. Owen gave him a thumbs-up. Patrick was far from being another Tim at the song, but he had a fair voice. Dressed in the altar boy's white surplice and red cassock, and with those rough-chapped breaker hands out of sight, he made a fine-looking chorister. Owen was about ready to see Thomas' bet and raise him, when the Hopmore No. 7 breaker whistle began shrilling. Rapid, short blasts, one after the other, on and on. They looked at each other and tossed their cards onto the table—a mine disaster.

CHAPTER TWENTY-SIX—Mine Fire

Maura came hurrying down the grassy hillside above the portal as the boys bolted from the shed. Farther on they ran past scattered shanties as women hurried outside wrapping their shawls about them. They sprinted the whole distance through town and were breathing hard as they got within sight of the mine. Smoke billowed up from the shaft and almost hid the breaker building. The fire company for the mine moved up a pump wagon and sluiced water onto the shaft head. Great pillows of white smoke rose, then yellow and red flashes of light flickered from the shaft, and more smoke roiled up and twisted into a smelly, black column. A horror took hold of everyone as word got around that men were trapped below, cut off from any escape by the burning shaft.

Liam caught Owen by the shoulder. "Go home and get our work things. They'll want a rescue team to bring out the workers as soon as the shaft fire is out," he said.

"What happened?"

"The hoist boss said the timbers above the furnace caught fire. It wasn't noticed until too late and only a few men made it out. Go now, and—"

He turned to see what had distracted Owen. People swarmed up the hillside from the direction of town. Aine hurried along in front, a cloth sack slung over her shoulder. When she reached them she swung her sack onto the ground and took a few seconds to catch her breath. "I thought you'd come here straight from town so I gathered up your work things," she said, staring at the column of flames and smoke, roaring and humming now like a forest fire climbing a mountain. "Will there be men below?"

"About forty," Liam said. "Men that didn't join our work stoppage."

"What chance will they have?"

"We hope some made it to the back of the mine and sealed themselves off from that poisonous smoke. If so, good, but they may not have much air left and we'll need to get to them soon."

Aine nodded, and touched Owen's shoulder. "Let me know if you need anything else from the house," she said to Liam. "I'll be waiting by that knoll. If you've not gone down by noon I'll walk back and get you both something to eat. Mind you keep safe, come what may." She went over to a nearby knoll to stand and watch with the other women.

Liam and Owen changed into work clothes and gumboots, and Owen joined his friends waiting near the shaft. The two volunteer fire companies from town rolled in, and their members at the No. 7 mine ran to join them. The three fire companies worked desperately to save the breaker building, but the flames ran wild up the walls. Another twenty minutes and the entire building glowed and sparked like the inside of a furnace. Parts of the burning building started collapsing onto the shaft and covered it over with flaming timber. Women on the hillside cried when it was clear no one would be able to enter the mine anytime soon.

The surface fires had almost burnt out by mid-afternoon. The fire companies trained their hoses to cool the smoldering mass of timber lying over the shaft head, and teams of mules were brought in to grapple and pull clear the charred pieces. Owen thought of his poor mules trapped below, and hoped it had been quick for them. Ian sprang to mind, and his stomach lurched. He'd gone in to work today. He prayed Ian had made it behind a barricade with the men.

By early evening the shaft head had been cleared of debris, but there were still fumes and stink rising from below. A large hand winch was skidded into place, and a lift platform was dragged up and rigged to the winch cable. A little black and white dog was tethered on the platform and lowered into the shaft. They let it to the bottom, waited, and brought it back up. The dog was unconscious when it reached the surface—maybe dead. The gases and smoke were still that bad. Maura clutched at Owen's sleeve and leaned her head on his shoulder.

A couple hours later a steam-driven bellows arrived on a wagon. It was used for ventilation at a smaller mine to the north, where a furnace wasn't suitable. The equipment was unloaded near the shaft and a mine engineer hurried to rig his steam engine to the bellows. Some coal was brought up from the rail cars at the siding and soon they had the engine going and the bellows pumping air. A fat hose line was attached to the bellows and the hose was lowered into the shaft. The initial blow-back from the shaft was smoky and smelled sickly, but it gradually cleared over the next hour. They sent down a cat in a wire basket, waited, and brought it back up, the cat a little unsteady but still meowing.

The call for rescue crew volunteers went out. Owen gave a thumbs-up to Maura and hurried over to join his da and the lines of men forming up. Peter fell in with them; he'd gone home at noon to eat lunch and had come back in his work clothes. The hand winch could handle only four or five men on the lift at one time, and Liam, Owen, and Peter went in on the fourth trip.

The air felt greasy and warm and Owen's eyes smarted after they'd lowered no more than fifty feet into the shaft. He watched as fingers of smoke trailed off charred nubs of timbers still hanging along the walls. The lift platform skipped and jogged downward as they cranked out more cable. They were maybe halfway down when a length of burnt timber fell from the shaft wall above, and bumped against the side of the lift as it hurtled by. The lift swung to the side and they held to each other as they hit the wall. A worker shouted from the tiny, lighted opening far above.

"Are you all right down there?"

It seemed no one knew quite what to answer, till a gruff voice called back up, "Keep lowering." And down they went.

Owen was glad to reach bottom and get off the lift. He and Peter climbed down a mound of burnt, smoldering rubble and moved away from the shaft, to form up with others waiting nearby. They were mostly a crew of laborers as far as Owen could see, but a couple of them were men his da had said were good as any miner they had. Those men and Liam led the way, and the rest followed carrying picks and shovels. Owen didn't look into the silent stables as they passed—he couldn't. They pulled the air hose along, with the men on top lowering it down the shaft to them until there was no more hose to let out. They waited then till an additional length was added at the top. Owen's ears rang, and it was hot and sweaty. Soon, throbbing pulses of fresh air started through the hose again. Not as much air pumped through the longer length, but they started forward again. Owen tried to breathe as little of the foul-smelling gases as possible, but his chest heaved with the need to suck in more oxygen.

They went farther back in the gangway and finally found where the miners had holed up. A flimsy wooden brattice leaned out from heaps of rubble and stone that had been piled against it from the other side. The trapped miners had tried to seal off gas leaks through the leaky brattice wall. The rescue crew pulled down the brattice to expose the rock and muck barrier heaped up behind it. They called to anyone who might hear on the far side. No sound, only a pulsing whoof of air from the ventilation hose, and the dripping water. They started digging.

Liam motioned Owen and Peter up onto the barrier. "They would've had a harder time stacking muck near the roof, so it'll likely be looser and have smaller pieces up there. Owen, take a hand at burrowing in at the top corner, and shove the muck back to Peter as you go in. The sooner we open up an airway through this the better."

Owen scrambled up to a toehold near the top and started throwing down rock. Peter got up next to him and waited while Owen bored in. As soon as Owen got partway in Peter reached in to take the rocks from him. It was hot and cramped by the time Owen stretched half his torso length into the hole. His miner's lamp grew dimmer and the air got warmer in the tight space. Sweat ran into his eyes and he coughed and choked on coal dust, but soon rocks began falling away from the far end of his burrow. He yelled back to Peter that he was through, then crawled out on the other side and waited for Peter to follow. Some workers passed them the air hose and they pulled it through the opening.

They crept down the far side of the barricade. Owen's lamp sputtered. The air reeked and he felt dizzy. A little farther back from the barricade dark forms lined both walls of the gangway. Some men sat leaning against the tunnel ribs, heads hanging askew, others sprawled on the floor, their faces buried in folded arms. More rocks loosened and slid down the face of the barricade as the rescue crew dug closer. Finally they broke through a central section of the barricade, and it became a little easier to draw a breath.

Owen watched the rescuers check some still figures, and go on to other men. He walked on, his mind numb, and he stopped when he saw Ian. He sat next to Deak, eyes open and vacant, and his head rested against Deak's shoulder. He and Deak held hands.

He heard Peter ask him if he'd known the kid next to Deak, but Owen couldn't say anything—he just nodded. Soon the men from the rescue crew had checked everyone--all dead-- and began picking up men from the floor. Owen leaned down, lifted Ian's arm around his shoulder, and stood with him. When he motioned toward Deak, Peter grimaced, but stooped to get him. They followed the line of men plodding toward the shaft.

The rescue workers layered the men two deep on the lift. When Peter went forward and laid Deak on the floor, Owen couldn't follow with Ian. There was no dignity to it at all. He shook his head and moved aside with Ian, unable to think what to do. Liam was behind him; he laid his man on the lift floor and motioned a couple of men forward with the bodies they carried. Then he had Owen step onto the lift, "Go up with your friend. Maybe you'll have a chance to hand him off to his ma. There's no great rush with what we've left to do down here."

The first streaks of daylight showed in the sky as they approached the top. The women surged against the line of railroad police when the lift cleared the surface, and they shouted and pointed at Owen standing with Ian. A ramp was laid to the platform and workers hurried on to carry away the bodies. Owen came off the lift still carrying Ian and the women surged around him. Shouting and weeping were everywhere. Some crying woman took Ian from him and others grabbed his arms and pulled at his jacket—would there be anyone else alive beside yourself? He kept telling them he was with the rescue crew, but they kept at him. He'd gotten clear when he saw Maura and the others hurry toward him.

"All you all right, then?" Maura said.

He nodded. "They're all dead," he said. "Every last one of them. I brought up a boy I worked with, Ian." The clean air had cleared off his headache, but he felt as tired and ill as someone with the fever. "They'll all be up soon. I'm going home."

Thomas and Patrick said they'd wait for Peter to come up, and Maura walked back with Owen. They didn't say much. It had been too terrible a night for that. He saw her home first, and then took the wagon trail and pathway to his own house. Aine was outside, waiting; she jumped up and took a pail of steaming hot water from the stovetop and added it to the cold in the tub. When he was ready she came to do his back.

"Did anyone survive?" she asked.

"No one. I carried up a boy I'd come to like pretty well, Ian, a Welsh kid. Gripping spirituality on him. Didn't win him any mercy, though. Just as dead as the others." It troubled him to say it, but there it went. "I can see why you don't go to church any more, mom."

She stopped rubbing his back and let the cloth drop into the tub. He turned to look at her standing straight with arms folded across her chest, looking off somewhere, light from the lantern wavering over her clenched figure. "Come away from that, Owen. I won't have my own peril become yours."

He couldn't turn away from watching her. She was like his da in that, risking God's anger with herself, but not wanting to lay that course for him.

CHAPTER TWENTY-SEVEN—Newspaper Apprentices

Owen slept till late in the morning. When he awoke he found da had not come home the night before, and he took a walk up to Kevin's. He told Kevin of the mine rescue attempt and they spent the rest of the day walking the old abandoned mines' route and talking out the tragedy.

That night was a fitful one for Owen, dreams of wandering in the darkness of the mine and coming upon the lighted face of Ian. Sometimes Ian sat against the mine rib looking as he was when they found him, other times he raced alongside Owen as his cart sped down the tracks out of control. Owen got up in the morning feeling as tired as when he went to bed. He and Liam ate breakfast together, and Aine gave them their lunch pails as if they were going off to a normal day of work. They didn't know what else to do and so they went.

What was left of the surface works looked even more depressing in the morning light. The charred hulk of the breaker building stood against the morning sun, with crisscrossed, splintered timbers sticking out of a blackened mass of debris. Part of the trestle leading away to the culm pile had burned and collapsed, leaving twisted steel rails dangling in the air. A sour, vinegary smell filled the warm air. The shaft collar area had been roped off and two men, dressed in suits, spoke with a group of mine bosses and the mine superintendent. Word went around that the mine might not open again for a long time. A terrible number of men, 36, had been lost, but there were twice that many still here and desperate for work.

When Liam left for town with his mates Owen joined his friends and walked back that way, too. Maura met them before they reached town.

"I was at a Mass this morning for the men who died," she said. "Fr. Morrison wants to see you."

"Isn't Sundays and confraternity enough? I'll see him then," Owen said.

"Och, ease up, Owen, he said it was something you'd be interested in."

Owen squeezed the back of his neck—felt like a bundle of twisted lift cables. He didn't want to hear any moral purpose for all those men dying like that. Still, he couldn't refuse Fr. Morrison. "Who's for walking up to the church with me?" he said. "He might not keep me so long if I've others waiting."

"I'll go," Maura said.

"Good enough showing, that," Peter said. "Best not to have too many of the faithful and invite a sermon. Anyway, I've still got the shakes from handling all those dead people. We'll look for you both at Kevin's tonight."

Maura and Owen left them at the corner and took the steep road up to the church. The morning was overcast and sultry, and they breathed deep by the time they got to the rectory. The housekeeper let them in and showed them into a small, darkened waiting room furnished with a bench and a few chairs set against the walls. Two old women were seated in there, people seeking help with living expenses. When Owen saw them waiting he started to leave, but Maura grabbed his arm and pulled him down beside her on a bench. They were there only a few minutes longer when Fr. Morrison leaned in at the doorway and motioned for Owen and Maura to come inside. They rose and Owen darted a glance at the women left waiting, but the one just smiled and the other stared ahead.

Fr. Morrison led the way and waved them into chairs. "A terrible tragedy for all," he said, settling behind his desk. "What can we possibly do but pray, ask for God's mercy, and give charity and consolation to the families left behind."

Owen slumped a little in his chair and watched him. Father's eyes were squeezed narrow and he fidgeted with a pencil. Owen hadn't noticed before how big his hands were, and the two mashed fingers. Had he always been a priest?

Fr. Morrison put down the pencil and brushed his hands back over his hair, holding them clasped behind his head for a moment. "I'm afraid there'll be even more pain and anguish ahead after we've buried our dead. We'll have men without work, and perhaps even more violence than we've already seen. I'm closer now to despair over a future for our young people. Look at you, both of you have worked hard to finish grammar school, and there should be more opportunities for you. Well then, at least I can speak of a job that might lead to a brighter future for yourself, Owen."

Owen twisted the corner of his mouth and folded his arms. Here it comes. Another try at recruitment for the seminary in Philadelphia.

Fr. Morrison went on. "You've no doubt heard of the efforts to organize a new union to represent the workmen. Mind you I've been against unions in the past, but seeing the cruel, unsafe conditions of employment as they've become I'm of a different mind now."

Owen bit the inside of his lip. Amazing. It was grand he'd finally come around to see some of the workmen's side of things. A little late, though.

"The new union organizers have decided to publish their own newspaper," Fr. Morrison said. "The Anthracite Journal, and I know the man selected for the job of editor. He's an old friend, and said he needs an apprentice to help at his newspaper. What do you think?"

Owen blinked; what was he talking about? "I'm looking to be a miner," he said.

Fr. Morrison drummed his fingers on the desk and shook his head. "Don't be so dense, lad. With the breaker burned to the ground and our mine closed there'll be another eighty or a hundred people out there today looking for a job. For God's sake this is a job. At least give it a try while you're looking to get on at another mine."

Owen knew he had answered more out of stubbornness than anything else. This was a chance to keep bringing home some money. He struggled to get out what he had to say. "Sorry, Father. I acted badly. For sure, I need the job. I'd like to go down to see your friend."

Fr. Morrison smiled and thumped his fist on the desk. He came from behind the desk to put an arm around Owen's shoulder. He told him his friend's name, and where the newspaper was being set up, in a long-vacant, wood joinery shop, over near the livery. He touched Maura's shoulder as she and Owen were about to leave and drew an envelope from inside his cassock.

"Your mother was by to see me. See that she gets this."

Maura was embarrassed to take it, but he pressed it into her hand. Her dad hadn't been well enough to go back to work yet.

They went down the hill and crossed through town to the newspaper office. Boxes were stacked on the wood-planked walkway in front of the office and the door stood open. They stepped inside and went up to a tall, sandy-haired man with a nose like a plowshare, and sleeves rolled up on pale, sinewy arms. He held a list and checked off boxes lined against a wall. He barely glanced at them, and returned his attention to his list.

"Mr. Grover Wilson?" Owen inquired.

"Yes?"

"Owen Dougherty, sir. Fr. Morrison sent me to ask you about an apprentice job."

He lowered his list and looked at Owen. "Oh yes, we spoke of you. A grammar school graduate, I understand. Why not secondary schooling?"

"I wanted to be a miner, sir. I worked in the mine as a mule driver, until the shaft fire. "

"A miner, is it? An admirable and honest craft, but hammered with danger, as we've just been reminded by this tragedy. I worked in a mine a few years myself, before going back to school. Fr. Morrison was one of my more spiritual-minded working mates when he left for the seminary. Did you know he was once a mine worker?"

Owen's eyes widened. "No sir. He never said." Owen had always respected Fr. Morrison, but now he leapt a notch higher in regard.

Grover had to be about six feet tall, topping Owen by a few inches, and had a continuous brown hedgerow for brows and clear blue eyes. "Well, Owen, we've suffered terrible losses at your mine because of poor safety, and safety is surely something a strong union would want improved. Did you know that there is already a law on the books that each mine must have a minimum of two separate entries for safety's sake? A prudent thought, but it costs money to sink a second shaft, so more often than not it's put off. Tell me, were you with the rescue team that went down?"

"Yes Sir, I was."

"Sit down at that desk and write something about the rescue effort, the men who participated, what you encountered, the men's reactions. I might be able to use your observations in an article I'll be writing on the mine safety situation. You might also show some useful writing ability. Generally you'd be helping with the more routine and mechanical chores of getting out a newspaper, of course, but there might be learning opportunities to draft material for the paper as well."

Owen felt for the edge of the desk to steady himself. "I'd like to do that," he said. He reached within for some extra confidence. "My friend, Maura, needs a job, too, if you can use another person." Grover turned and looked at her. Owen worried he'd overstepped, but then figured what harm was there in the asking? He added, "She and I worked together to produce a yearbook for our graduating class." Maura flushed a vivid red, and Owen nodded some encouragement at her. The yearbook was just an eight-page, gel-duplicator job, but it was nicely done, and experience was experience. Grover's long, granite face, accented by that nose, crinkled a little as he studied Maura.

"Did you sell any advertising space for your yearbook?" he asked.

Maura stammered, but got it out, "Oh, yes Sir, two pages of advertising from local merchants—maybe a dozen, no, perhaps ten. And I signed them up myself."

"Well, some business acumen, then. I could have you accompany me on the first round of soliciting advertisements for the newspaper. Afterward we could do monthly visits, and record any new ad content the merchants wanted. That, and helping out with printing tasks might provide ample involvement for a part-time job with the paper. We'll see how it goes—sound satisfactory?"

"Oh, indeed," Maura said, beaming. "Thank you, Sir."

Grover told them what the starting pay would be, which was at least better than breaker wages, and they were glad to agree. Owen sat at the desk in the storefront writing what he remembered of the rescue details, while Grover and Maura carried boxes inside. The words came easy enough to Owen as he recalled all the events, from when they'd first heard the warning whistle, to feeling in his stomach the weight of the disaster as he watched the flames, and right to the end when he carried up Ian. He tried to describe the complicated workings of a mine, so that someone who'd never been in one might understand what had happened. When details seemed too much, he'd start that part over. The afternoon sun glinted through the plate glass window and squares of light moved across his paper. He'd rewritten the first page once, but afterward he just lined through stuff he wanted to change. It seemed no time at all till he had four pages of writing.

After Grover and Maura finished moving the cartons in and shifting things around, he came over and sat at the edge of Owen's desk. Owen stacked the finished pages together, handed them off, and hurried to finish his last page. Grover took a pencil from a jar on the desk and made notations as he read. Owen handed him the last page and he marked that, too.

"Good flow, some useful detail," he said. "It can be tightened up to better effect, as I've shown in my markup. Take the article and pad with you and try doing a rewrite tonight. Let Maura do some proofreading after you're through. It helps to have a fresh eye looking at writing in progress."

He went on to talk about the newspaper he figured on building, the types of things he was interested in covering, and the important role the paper could play in helping the cause of the workingman. Maura and Owen listened, mouths open, jaws slack. Finally Grover pulled out a pocket watch from his vest and flicked it open. "Early closing today," he said, "I've got to cover a union organizing meeting. It's been hard for the union to find neutral ground for this meeting, what with the fierce ethnic differences around here and the railroad opposition to a union, but they've settled on using the horse auction shed behind the livery. I'll see you both back here in the morning, eight o'clock."

CHAPTER TWENTY-EIGHT— Trust

They left the office feeling grand about getting the newspaper job. Owen considered the pluses. It wasn't like he'd be getting his own mining chamber to work, but he'd be sticking close to mining until he could get back in. The Journal would deal with lots of things that interested miners. Sure, there'd be other news and politics, but from what Grover had said, there'd be stories of how the different mines worked to get their coal out, the new tools and equipment miners used, safety concerns, union organizing, all sorts of great stuff.

"We could start working on that article right away," he said as they walked through town. "Let's go up to the winch shed at the Monroe; we've got the table, the benches, and there's still some good light to work by."

"Grand. I've a stack of things I was supposed to do at home, but they can wait. I've an official job now," Maura said.

The afternoon turned cooler as a weak sun lowered into the gray thunderheads above the mountains. They reached the mine at almost four o'clock. Walking across the top of the culm pile, Owen tapped Maura's shoulder and pointed west. A distant curtain of rain slanted down from the clouds and hid the far peaks. They continued on to the shed and lifted open the rickety door.

Maura said, "I'm going to explore outside while you study Grover's notes and work on your article. Call me when you're ready and I'll come in and read it."

"Okay, that'll be good. I'll go through his comments again and have a couple of pages ready for you to start reading soon enough."

The air felt close inside, and Owen used an iron bar to prop open the cable flap door. He spread out the four pages on the table and studied the types of notations Grover had used. Some were no harder to understand than a marked-up English composition paper, others took some guessing. He sat down with the pad and started writing, glancing at his original as he went along. The writing went quickly at first, but slowed when he tried to describe the terrors of seeing all the dead workers. Gradually, the room grew darker and he looked up from his writing. The rain must be moving closer now. Outside the window, flashes of lightning stabbed through the sky and thunder boomed near.

A shriek jarred his thoughts. He jumped up from the table, knocked over the bench, and ran outside. Maura was nowhere to be seen and he yelled for her. The answering call came from somewhere inside the mine. He ran down the decline and met her walking up, drenched and dripping water.

"It's flooded at the bottom and I fell in," she said.

Owen almost laughed, she looked so pathetic, but an angry frown on her face warned against it. They walked up the ramp to the portal and found it pouring rain outside. Maura kept walking right out into the downpour. As soon as she was inside the shed Owen ran for it. The rain brought with it a sudden coolness and Maura held her arms clasped tightly about her chest and shivered. Owen loaded some coal pickings and wood kindling into the boiler furnace, took down the canister of matches, and got a small fire going.

"We'll keep the furnace door open and pull a bench over. You can take off your dress and lay it out on the bench to dry."

"Take off my dress?" She shouted. "With you here?"

"Maura, you're soaking wet. What's the matter—are you worried about me?"

She frowned and stared hard, hesitated, then undid her belt, crossed her arms to catch the dress on both sides, and up and over it went. He had wondered if she'd take such a dare. She stood in a white slip, her dark hair splayed about bare shoulders, and Owen blinked. He hadn't thought Maura had much, but the thin, wet slip showed to good effect. He pulled a bench close to the furnace, stretched out her dress and his own shirt on it, and Maura put her shoes on the floor in front of the furnace. They stood close behind the bench, watching the flames, and listening to the rusted, empty boilerplates creak and pop as they heated. He put his arm around her and she leaned her head against his shoulder. He turned her to face him and they kissed. The only sounds for the next couple of minutes were the boiler noises and the rain drumming on the roof. They moved clumsily against each other, and almost fell over the bench.

"Do you want to go lie down on the tarp behind here," he said, and twisted up his mouth when he remembered. What would they do about the crucifix?

Maura breathed hard. "I guess we've already sinned if we thought about it. Did you?"

"I did."

She broke into a fit of shivers and he held her more tightly. He said, "We'd have more than that sin to handle if something came of it. So, we'd better wait, right?"

"Right," she said, and stopped shaking so much.

CHAPTER TWENTY-NINE—Arrested

Owen handed his revised copy to Grover the next morning. Grover laid it on his desk and got Owen and Maura busy opening wooden crates of used printing press equipment, type sets, inkpads, and other supplies that he'd had shipped from Philadelphia. They were busy all day setting up the equipment, and near the end of the day Grover sat at his desk reading Owen's article. He called Owen over.

"It's well improved," he said. "I'll talk tomorrow with some of the miners you've mentioned by name and sound them out on safety issues. I'd like to have their views of the old union's efforts toward safety, and how our new union might better deal with it. I'll work some of your material into our first issue—it's due out next week. You have a stirring firsthand account of the rescue effort that I can work with, and it'll lead right into planning my interviews on the disaster and safety problems." He reached to take down a book from a shelf above the desk. "Here's a style guide. Refer to it for explanations of notations I've used in my editing."

Owen took the book and he and Maura left for home. It had been strange to him, working all day in an office with daylight streaming in at all the windows. But no use denying it, he'd missed some of the thrills of working in a mine. Sure, but what if he was ever injured and his faith in God was put to the test? There were reminders of such trials all around. The man over there sitting in a wheel chair outside the barber shop, missing both legs. A man on crutches, one pants leg pinned up, clumping along ahead of them. A guy this morning, leaning against a shop front and holding a bag under his chin while he struck a match with his good arm. They had all been mineworkers, once. He wondered if they still prayed?

He stopped and idled with Maura at a fork in the trail leading up to her shanty. The closeness they'd reached at the shed yesterday was a powerful thing. A blessed sign of wisdom that they'd gone only that far and no farther—or they might have been worried sick now. Instead, they could relax and smile at each other.

He was in good spirits when he came off the trail and onto the path to his house. It was short-lived, though. He knew something was wrong when he saw Aine sitting on the steps by the garden. She was usually busy cooking a meal at this hour, and heating water. He put his book in the house and came out to sit beside her. She stayed looking out toward the hills.

"What do you see out there?"

"I don't know—emptiness." She tightened her arms about her chest, bent over to stifle a small cry, and straightened again. "They took your da away."

Owen caught his breath and his stomach knotted. "When? Who?"

"Just a while ago. He'd only stepped inside the house when men rushed up and forced their way inside. The police, and some other armed men. They struck him when he tried to speak with me and dragged him off."

Owen let out his breath. The failing light of sundown was slipping away from the valleys. "I'd almost made myself believe nothing would happen to da," he said, trying hard to keep his words steady. He looked beside him at Aine, still staring beyond, hands clasped across drawn-up knees, tension lines tugging at the corner of her eye.

She said, "I didn't think I'd be so destroyed. What will become of him?"

This time Owen couldn't trust his voice. He just shook his head, got up and touched her on the shoulder, and climbed the stairs.

Owen spent a fearful night of twisting and turning in bed, awake for hours, sinking into brief, fitful starts of sleep, and wracked by dreams too horrid to be recalled. He woke in a sweat, and resolved to try visiting his da at jail that day. On their way to work Owen told Maura about his da's arrest. She was shocked and upset, but he couldn't bring himself to talk at any length about it. When they got to the newspaper office Grover wasn't in yet, and Maura used her key to enter. A dozen hinged cases of used, dirty type sets were waiting to be cleaned. They each took an end of the worktable and emptied the cases onto the surface. Owen raised a couple of window sashes to get a cross-draft going and he filled their trays with solvent. Working hard would keep his mind busy with something beside a growing sense of doom. Grover came in about ten o'clock carrying his briefcase, and called Owen over.

"I heard about your father's arrest. Keep up your courage. They've arrested another six men, besides. A couple of others they were after must have gotten word and fled before being apprehended."

"What will happen now?" Owen said.

"They'll be taken before a judge today, to be charged, and to enter a plea. The railroad seems anxious to get more cases underway while public fears have been aroused over the wave of killings. The big city newspapers claim a vast Molly Maguire conspiracy stretches over this entire country and abroad."

"Do you believe that?"

He shook his head. "No, it's far-fetched speculation, but it commands attention and sells newspapers. I suspect there are probably not more than a couple hundred Mollies, and mostly here in Schuylkill County. Maybe only a part of them were involved in the mine assassinations and violence. They might have thought theirs was the only way, but they'd be wrong. Violence will never solve our labor troubles."

"If they're convicted, do you think they'll—" He couldn't finish it.

Grover watched him for a few seconds. "If the Tully trial is any indication the prosecutor and his battery of lawyers will dominate the trial and they'll demand a hanging. We'll soon know how effective they were; Tully's case will go to the jury today."

Owen turned and walked toward the door. Grover signaled to Maura to go after him. She caught up with Owen walking along the block of storefronts.

"It would be quiet up in the church this time of morning," she said. "We could go up and say a prayer that your da will come through

201

this all right."

"I don't think prayer ever changes anything. God just lets it all happen. I'm not going into church to plead on my knees. Da wouldn't, and I won't either."

"We could just walk, then. Do you want to go up into the hills?"

"You'd better go back to work, Maura. It's a good job. I just can't keep my mind on anything right now. If he fires me, I'll get on at another mine somewhere around here."

"All right, then. I'll go back. But we can say a few prayers even while we're up and about, right?"

"You don't give up easily, do you? Maybe there's nothing else left to do. I'm going to see if they'll let me visit my da at the jail. If they won't, I'll go up to Kevin's."

The jailhouse was a sandstone block addition built onto the rear of the wood courthouse. Owen became nervous going up the entry steps, but the door was open and he resolved to get on with it. Inside a sergeant of the Coal and Iron Police leaned on a long counter, reading a newspaper. A scale-model of a railroad car, heaped full with pieces of coal, stood farther along on the countertop. After a few minutes the sergeant looked up.

"What is it you want, lad?"

"I'd like to visit my da, Liam Dougherty."

"Dougherty, is it? He's to have no visitors until our detectives are through questioning him."

Owen's jaw tightened. "But when will that be?"

The sergeant went back to reading the paper. "Maybe after his trial."

CHAPTER THIRTY—The Test

Owen and Kevin sat outside at a round table sawn from the thick trunk of a chestnut tree. Looking out across a low hedge, the far view was hemmed in by steep slopes all around. A few high clouds strung out over the hills and the air was cool. Owen told Kevin of the latest happenings and Kevin shook his head but kept his usual, thoughtful look.

He said, "Grover's right to work around any violence, but he's foolish to waste any time at all in fighting against the mine owners."

Owen frowned. "Where's the sense of that, Kevin? There'd never be any justice won for the workers."

"People are too quick to bet their lives on getting their own idea of justice done. The truth is there isn't any justice in this world, never will be. Look for the best non-violent way you can find to get by, and don't get yourself killed doing it."

Owen grimaced. Kevin might be a souper, but he'd make a blessed saint, too. The three of them, his da, Grover, and Kevin were all at odds on where to stand in this fight. His da and Kevin seemed to be on opposite extremes, but Grover seemed to hold to some middle ground, and maybe he could steer everyone that way. That shouldn't be too much to hope for. They had a lunch of bread and tea and Owen went back down the hill and on to the courthouse.

The courthouse, jail, and mayor's office were all in one building, a long, steep-roofed, wood framed structure. The trial was in progress when Owen stepped through the front doors and he eased them closed again as he looked around. Grover was easy enough to spot in his crumpled tan jacket, no tie, hair standing up like a wheat shock. He sat taking notes at the front, off to one side of the judge and facing the jury across the room. Owen worked his way behind Grover, out of his line of sight. The judge had finished his instructions and told the prosecution side to begin their summation.

The prosecutor was a hefty, balding man wearing a black waistcoat, and a broad tie that looked like a brown silk muffler. He strutted over in front of the jury box and waved his pair of folded spectacles in the air.

"You are asked," he almost shouted, "by a beleaguered society to take a first step in bringing a ruthless band of bloodthirsty, obdurate, hellish fiends to the bar of justice. You are being called upon to help us sear out the cancerous growth of Molly Maguirism from within our midst. Return this horde, beginning with this murderous devil before you, back to the Prince of Darkness from whence he sprang."

Owen listened, alarmed. He seemed to be saying just evidence of even being a Molly should be enough to hang a man. The Germans in the jury seats looked wide-eyed at the blustering prosecutor. The ones in the front row pulled in their chins as he passed, shouting and swinging his spectacles like a sickle. The jurors' closed expressions never changed as the prosecutor roared in language that sounded one minute like a Civil War speech, and the next minute like a church sermon on the harrowing fires of Hell. Owen watched the faces of the jurors. Who knew how much the Germans even understood? He couldn't catch it all himself. Afterward, he caught a look at Crimp's smirking face as the defense summed up its case. The defense lawyer attacked, trying to show Crimp as lying and having made a deal with the prosecutor to save himself. Owen rubbed his jaw—are they going to see it? The jury faces looked as blank as wiped slates.

When the lawyer finished and the jury adjoined to decide Tully's fate, Owen slipped out of the courtroom. He waited across the street as people came out to gather in front of the courthouse. More people began arriving and they hurried inside while a dozen railroad police armed with rifles formed a line out front. Owen grew anxious; they must be getting ready to bring in the other Mollies for trial. He walked back across the street.

"What business have you here?" a policeman said as he started up the stairs.

"I work for the Anthracite Monitor," Owen said. "I have a message for our editor inside."

The policeman glanced up and down at Owen's rough work clothes, took a long, hard look at his face, and let him pass. Owen hurried inside and a few minutes later some guards and prisoners entered from the rear. Liam was one of the last to come in, and when the prisoners filed into the front row of seats he sat on the outside. Owen hurried down the aisle and sat in an empty seat behind him.

"Da, it's me. Are you all right?"

Liam turned his head slightly. A small flicker of a smile, and he nodded. The guard patrolling the aisle shoved Owen's shoulder back onto his chair.

"There's to be no speaking with the prisoners. What are you

about?"

"He's my da," Owen said.

"This isn't a prisoners visiting room," he snapped.

"Sorry," Owen murmured. The policeman glared at him and turned away.

After a few minutes the same prosecutor from Tully's trial got up, leaned on the table, and read from papers lying in front of him. He described one of the assassinations that happened at the beginning of the year, gave the names of the men accused, and a list of the charges. Liam and three other men were made to stand, and their lawyer gave pleas of not guilty. The prosecutor was reading details of a second assassination when the same policeman tapped Owen on the shoulder. The detective, Buell, stood beside him.

"Come along," the policeman said. "We want to talk with you."

Owen went stiff as a mine prop. Buell smiled down at him and his panic increased.

"Am I going to yank you out of that seat or are you coming with us?" the policeman said.

Liam turned with a worried look. Owen got up and went with them, his heart pounding. They went out the front door of the courtroom and around the hallway to the jail at the rear. They took him to a small office room, and the policeman waited outside while Buell closed the door behind them. A battered wood desk and a couple of chairs were at one end of the room and benches lined the walls around the other three sides. Crimp lay on his back on one of the benches, head resting on clasped hands, legs drawn up. He smiled when he saw them, swung his feet down, and sat up.

"Sure, I remember that one with his da from a few times before," Crimp said. "He'd be a one to suspect, all right."

"Perhaps," Buell said, motioning Owen to a chair before his desk. He went around to the other side and took a seat. Buell clasped his bony white fingers on the desktop and seemed to wait for Owen to speak. Crimp drew up a chair beside Owen and straddled it, sitting backwards. He leaned with arms resting on the chair back and grinned at Owen. After a few seconds Buell reached into a waistcoat pocket and drew out a piece of paper. He unfolded it, and smoothed it on the desktop.

"We found this list in your father's possession. The list contains the names of suspected Mollies who were implicated in past crimes, including men we'd planned to arrest in raids last night.

Unfortunately, several among them had already fled, and so avoided arrest. Now then, Owen, aiding and abetting criminals is a serious crime, and whoever had a hand in raising an alarm for those men might spend a long time in prison. I'd like to know who prepared this list, and where they got their information. Can you tell us anything that may help?"

Owen's voice didn't work at first and he had to make a second start. "No, sir," he said.

"I see. So what, exactly, do we know here? One, the list appears to be written in an educated, cursive style. Two, the so-called coffin notices posted by the Mollies are all crudely spelled and printed. And Three, we find your father can barely print his own name. Now where might all that lead us?"

"I don't know," Owen said. Sunlight slanted in from narrow closed windows at the top of a wall, and the air in the room lay warm and still. Owen kept swallowing.

"Let's go on, then. We've uncovered the interesting fact that you have a grammar school diploma, unusual for coal patch boys, and commendable," Buell said. He leaned back and pulled a desk drawer open. He groped inside and produced a pencil and a sheet of paper, which he laid on the desk in front of Owen. "I'm going to read names from our list, and I want you to write them in cursive on this sheet of paper. Shall we begin?"

Owen blinked some sweat from his eyes and nodded. Crimp snickered and nodded for him to take up the pencil. Buell read from the list while Owen wrote. When he was through, Buell took the list and compared it with the one he held. He studied them for a few, long minutes. Owen grew nervous; maybe he wrote like Maura. Finally Buell frowned, folded both sheets, and tucked them away in his waistcoat. A prosecution lawyer popped his head through the doorway.

"The jury is back—they found Tully guilty," he said. "A quick verdict of the people, hey? Our Krauts might not have understood all the testimony but they got all the appearances right. The judge set a hanging for the beginning of next month. Tully won't be alone, though. I expect there'll be others ready to swing by then, too."

Buell nodded to him and faced Owen again. "That will be all," he said. "You're free to go—for now."

CHAPTER THIRTY-ONE—Jail Visit

Sunday morning Owen woke early when he heard Aine moving about. He'd had another restless night and didn't get much sleep. He dressed, went outside and took a chair by the stove, and Aine brought over tea and oatmeal. He told her about seeing da. She stiffened when she heard of the sentence given Tully, and stopped work every few minutes to stand with a hand against her forehead, covering her eyes. Owen avoided telling her about the trouble of the Molly list.

After Aine had left for a walk up to her refuge, Owen had to decide what to do next. He'd heard at the courthouse that the railroad planned to reopen the Hopmore No. 7, but the shaft and entry had to be cleared of burned timbers to help evaluate total costs. They wanted to hire temporary day laborers to get the work done. Owen doubted he still had any job with the newspaper, so maybe he'd try getting one of the shaft cleanup jobs.

The sky was a dim gray when he left the house. He was uneasy about skipping church but he was getting more like his mom, even if she didn't want to hear him say it. You had to deal with life as best you could, and the Church and the sacraments weren't going to give much help. Not now.

There weren't many people going about as he went through town, and he fell in with some men walking toward the mine. Tomorrow maybe he'd look for a regular job at a mine over in Shamokin. The miner wasn't as much his own man any more, but it was still hard to give up that goal. The owners would like nothing better than to run the mines like factories, and things might just be headed that way. What else was left? He booted a stone to the side of the road.

The air at the mine still had the sour smell of wet and charred timber. All of the breaker debris had been dragged back from the shaft collar. A mine boss holding a clipboard assembled the day laborers next to a new tag board. He asked a few questions of each man to judge his experience, and after hiring someone gave them a temporary work tag to place on the board. Those who had already worked at the mine and showed their old tag were hired straightaway. Owen went down with the first crew, equipped with steel cables and winches to drag the wreckage of the ventilating furnace from its shaft pocket. Another crew worked from the lift platform inside the shaft, barring down the burned timber sets.

The work of handling the burned timbers was slow and dangerous, and the day passed slowly. Sorting through the ruins of a much-needed workplace cast a pall over the men and they spoke only when it was needed. At Noon, Owen realized he'd forgotten to pack a lunch, and he sat off by himself, brooding about his da's plight and fearful of what was coming.

By the time he arrived back home that evening he was filthy black. Aine took one look and had him sit on the bench while she went for another few buckets of water. She doused him with a first, cold rinse, helped him sponge away the layers of soot, and he got into the warm tub. He'd easily have fallen asleep if she hadn't come around every few minutes to check on him.

"You didn't go to church today," Aine said, as she scrubbed his back.

He waited till she paused scrubbing, and he said, "You neither."

The brush dropped and he turned to glance over his shoulder. Her eyes glared.

"And haven't you always known why it is I don't go? As bitter and angry today as when they told me my two sons were killed for some glorious cause—how would I go to church anymore?" she shouted at him.

The abiding, invisible presence of the one son, especially, seemed to weigh on Owen. "You lost your favorite son back then, but you still have me. I love you a lot, and I'm trying hard as I can to get you to love me as much."

She was quiet, and he didn't dare turn around to look her in the face again. A couple million years blew past.

"Stand up," she said.

He winced, but stood and stepped out of the tub to one side, his back to her. She didn't pour it slow—just deluged him in one swoop. He heard the bucket hit the ground rolling, and when he wiped the water from his eyes, saw her walking away. He sluiced water from his torso. He'd finally said it, but he wished she had hit him over the head with the bucket afterward.

Owen met his friends at Kevin's that evening. They'd missed him at church and were surprised to hear he'd worked the day. Patrick was hired as a breaker boy at a nearby mine and started tomorrow. When Thomas and Peter applied they were told to come back later in the week. The mine hoped to sell more coal, now that the

Hopmore No. 7 had closed, but they needed additional time to develop new chambers.

"Thomas and I are going to try a couple mines over by Shamokin, tomorrow," Peter said. "Want to go? We can catch a ride with a wagonload of workers that goes that way every morning."

"I guess so; do you think I'd have a chance for another underground job?"

"Might be tough for a young Mick from outside moving right into one of those spots," Peter said.

"What's the matter with coming back to the newspaper?" Maura said. "I think Grover expects you back."

"Even after I walked out like that?"

"Owen, he knew you were upset over your da's arrest. He spotted you at the court yesterday and hoped you'd show up at the newspaper office in the afternoon. I had to help him set type till ten o'clock last night, and we still need a load of work done to get out a first edition this week."

Owen sipped his tea. It was from Kevin's private stock, dark as coal and smoky tasting. Someone sent him a box every year. Anyhow, who'd visit his da if he didn't? Probably not his mom. If Grover really would let him come back, he'd better jump on it. "I'll give it a try, Maura. I hope you're right."

The next day He went in with Maura. Grover acted as if Owen had only taken a day off and was coming back to work as expected. Owen was thankful for that. There were things he would have liked to ask Grover—about Tully's conviction, and what that might mean for Liam—but there was no time. That was okay, too; better to work hard than to think about things you couldn't change. Grover rushed them from one task to another, sometimes forgetting they needed more than a brief sketch of what to do next. Maura was too sensitive to go back and ask questions, but Owen would do it. You needed to learn right the first time, but you also needed a decent first time.

By the end of the day Owen's back and neck muscles felt in knots. He and Maura left the newspaper office when it started getting dark. Owen decided he'd try again to visit his da, and Maura wanted to go with him to the jailhouse. Owen convinced her he had a better chance of getting in to see him if he went alone.

As he walked along the streets a squad of uniformed cavalry from the state's Easton Regiment galloped past. There'd been more arrests made the previous night over at Shamokin, and the railroad raised an alarm that a large force of Mollies might try to free the prisoners. They seemed to want people believing there was this army of Mollies threatening the countryside.

Owen stopped and flattened into a shop doorway just as Fr. Morrison came out of the alleyway next to the courthouse. He turned when he reached the street boardwalk and walked the other way. Owen waited a minute, then hurried along to the alley.

The same sergeant was at the desk. "What is it, lad?"

"I'd like to visit a few minutes with my da, Liam Dougherty, sir."

He studied Owen. "You again. Your da, is it? I suppose you must know all about him being a Molly Maguire?"

"No, sir. I just want to visit with him."

"Wait here a minute," he said. He came out from behind the counter, walked down a hallway, and knocked at a door. When it opened the sergeant spoke to someone inside and gestured with a nod toward Owen. Buell stepped into the hallway and smiled. He walked up to Owen and extended a hand. Owen hesitated, and shook hands with him. Buell tucked his thumbs into his waistband and regarded him for a few seconds.

"I believe that list has caused us further problems, Owen. We moved as quickly as possible to arrest some remaining suspects near Shamokin last night, but we found that another two had absconded." Buell raised a hand to his face and rubbed at whisker stubble with the tips of his fingers. The puzzle of the list still bothered him. Owen swallowed; he was glad Maura hadn't come with him. Suppose Buell thought to have another known graduate take a writing test.

"Take him back to see his father," Buell said to the sergeant.

They had the eight suspected Mollies crowded together in two cells. The sergeant had a jailer take Liam out of his cell and locked him and Owen together in a smaller, empty cell. Liam looked haggard, like he hadn't washed or shaved since he'd been arrested. They gave each other quick hugs and mumbled greetings.

"I saw Fr. Morrison on his way out," Owen said.

"Yes, he was here for confessions and to warn us we must atone for our sins. So that you know, Owen, I do fear how God may judge me, and I was glad of a chance to speak of my doubts in private confession to a priest. Still, Fr. Morrison would have us also make a public admission of guilt and appeal for the public's forgiveness, but that I will not do. The Mollies fought back in the only way left to mineworkers. If anyone is to be in a prisoner's dock, the mine owners should be there."

"Da, did you know the jury had Jim Tully guilty, and the judge sentenced him to hang?"

They looked at each other as the rattling and voices of the jailhouse went on outside the cell. Liam appeared more tired than fearful. The wiry steel gray hair was like a tattered burr patch, and his once bold moustache seemed an aged thing. His eyes had the lifeless blue of a rainy sky. He said, "Yes, and it could go the same way for me, Owen."

Owen had to sit down on a bench. He kept brushing his hand through his hair and shaking his head. The air in the place was suffocating. When he figured he could talk again he asked, "Do they have people that are going to testify against you—like Crimp?"

"Not him, but another breed of informer—a detective spy working for the railroad. James McParlan, an Irishman, who pretended to be an out-of-work miner and joined our ranks. He argued for one of the bosses' assassinations, and we see now his purpose was to trap any who might participate. McParlan is set to testify I was one of the leaders who approved the action. If so he could have warned the mine boss beforehand, but then that wouldn't have suited his purpose."

Owen slumped against the bars behind him. What hope was left?

"Time!" the jailer rapped the bars with his baton as he walked past the cell.

"How's your mother? Have you found any work?" Liam said.

The jailer was already opening the door as Owen struggled with soreness in his throat. "Mom's fine. I got a job as a journalist's apprentice. The new mine worker's union is going to publish their own newspaper."

Liam smiled and squeezed Owen's shoulder, and the jailer took Liam back to the holding cell.

CHAPTER THIRTY-TWO—The Verdict

The eight Mollies arrested were separated into two groups for trial. One trial was to be in Hopmore, and the other was moved to a small town up north, in Roseburg. The proceedings got started at the end of the month and Liam was to be tried with the Mollies at Hopmore. Grover's last editorial had been about the rush to trial. He told readers perhaps the railroad was worried about efforts of the new union to organize the mineworkers, and wanted the Mollies out of the way before they took on the new union. He said prospects were poor that the accused men would get a fair and just trial.

Grover was away from the newspaper office for most of the week, taking part in union organizing meetings at Hopmore and Shamokin. He worked with Owen and Maura in the pressroom the entire day before publication so they could get the paper out on time. There were some disasters, a column and several paragraphs misplaced, and small errors scattered about. Owen did more than his share of making errors, but they propped him up through it all, a few minutes of talk to distract him when he looked terrible, a smile often enough—it all helped.

Grover took Owen with him to Liam's trial the following week. Owen learned a little more about courtroom strategies from Grover while they were there, but it was hard to take his eyes from da's face through it all. He could not read much in it. Liam had shut away any sign of feelings.

Owen's worries over da increased steadily during the trial. He tried to follow it all. The railroad lawyers never offered any motive for why the Mollies might have committed their crimes—they did it simply because they were bloodthirsty creatures. And if the Mollies' lawyers brought up any connection with labor injustice, it was knocked down by the judge—out of order, stick to the charges. In all the legal skirmishes the railroad lawyers split the seam with rapid, tight shots, while the defense lawyers seemed to be using damp powder that sputtered to no avail at all.

Owen got his first look at McParlan several days into the trial; thin, small ears, huge moustache, and wearing smallish, round steel wire spectacles. The defense lawyers showed McParlan indeed pushed for one of the assassinations, and was there when it was carried out. Still, the prosecution lawyers claimed an undercover agent was immune from any charges of complicity. Owen shivered when McParlan said he heard Liam and another man order the assassination. Other evidence McParlan gave was only what a few

Mollies had told him, and which he read from entries in his journal. Owen studied the faces of the jury during the testimony. Who could say what they might have thought of such evidence? Did the Dutchmen even understand what McParlan had said?

When Owen got home that evening Aine was sitting outside on the bench, her eyes closed and her back leaned against the wall of the oven, the firebox open and cold. No need to start daily baths for two working mine laborers any more. Still, she'd never missed having his supper on. He went over and touched her shoulder. She turned to look at him, jumped up, and hurried about gathering kindling and shoving it into the firebox. He tried to get her to stop, told her he wasn't hungry, but she kept at it till she had a ripping fire going. When the lid of the water kettle started rattling she filled a teapot, then thumped a wad of soda bread dough into a pan.

All the activity, the stifling warmth around the oven, the hopelessness of another day of waiting to see what would happen—he wandered down the hillside to sit near the garden. The air stirred just a little, and it became a little easier to breathe. He couldn't bear to look out on all the open space beyond, thinking about his da locked up in that ugly little cell. A few minutes later his mom came down the steps. She sat beside him and handed him a mug of tea. They sat quietly for a few minutes.

"I think he's always tried to do what he thought was right," Owen said. "Like sending Ben and Sean off to fight for the Union, and—" He had to stop a minute to think. "And helping the mineworkers in their fight. Even when it meant—" He forced himself to finish it, "being part of the assassinations." He looked beside him. Aine drew deep, measured breaths, her mouth trembling a little, and she got to her feet. She touched him on the shoulder and climbed the stairs.

The trial finished on a Thursday, four weeks after it began. Owen thought there was a chance they hadn't convinced the jury, but they were out only an hour longer than Tully's jury, and they voted guilty. He didn't remember much of what went on after the foreman read the verdict. People cheered in the courtroom while Liam and the other Mollies were shackled to each other and led away. Owen went back to the newspaper office with Grover. He told Maura and she broke down and cried. She wanted to go home with him that evening, to be there when he had to tell Aine, but he said there was no need for that.

Owen walked slowly down the path, and Aine stood rigidly watching him come. He'd told her in the morning that the trial would end that day, and that the jury might reach a quick verdict. When she saw it in his face she slammed down the long-handled wooden peel onto a shelf beside the oven, jerked the bubbling water kettle off the stove plate, and banged it down on a trivet. She stood with fists clenched against her hips, and looked away to the hills. He started to tell her about the verdict, and saw the glint of sunlight reflect from the small window next to the door, saw now the small porcelain statue of the Infant of Prague back in its place. He turned from the statue and looked at her. He'd thought maybe she had been wonderfully strong, not needing all those relics, and icons, and statues, and Masses, to plead against things they had to face on their own.

"They found him guilty," she said, assuming it, in short, clipped words.

He hurt so badly he wanted to hurt her too. "Yes, that's how it went, so you can put away your statue now."

She kept her steady, measured breaths, and blanketed any explosions within. She shook her head, tossed a towel she was holding onto the oven bench, and walked from the yard. Owen sat on the bench and cried.

The next day, the judge sentenced his da and the others to hang.

CHAPTER THIRTY-THREE—The Parting

The following day the four prisoners were transferred north to Roseburg, which had a medium-size prison. They were to be hanged there along with the other four accused Mollies who were convicted in Roseburg.

None of Owen's days seemed real to him any more. He kept working because his mother and he needed the money to survive, and he also needed something to keep his mind off what was happening. He and his mom didn't talk much, his depression kept him from even trying, and the statue stayed in the window. He looked at it often, shaking his head. Maybe she thought it could still win some help from the Almighty, but he was done with all that. They'd asked God's help and none came. It didn't have to turn out this way, but it did. He'd live the rest of his life without asking God for anything.

After a few weeks had gone by Grover returned from a trip to Roseburg and told Owen he'd be able to go up now and visit his da. Owen took a day off from work and caught a ride on a freight wagon leaving town early the next day. After a teeth-jarring, bone-bruising ride of more than fifteen miles he thanked the driver and found his way to the prison. He hadn't expected to find it so large a place, and right within the town, flanked by a couple of rooming houses, a hotel, and some shops. A guard wrote him out a pass at the front gate and he walked through a yard area toward the main building. He slowed when he noticed all the sawing and hammering going on in the prison yard. His chest tightened; a gallows platform, for sure, and he forced himself to keep walking toward the main building.

His da was in a cell with another Molly. A priest was with the other man, reading to him from a prayer book. His da sat on the edge of his cot and Owen drew up a stool near him. Da nodded toward the other prisoner, "It's his turn with his own pastor. Fr. Morrison was here to see me yesterday. He's come a few times, even though the once for a last confession would have been enough for me."

"Did you tell him that?"

"I did, but he's still hoping I'll make a public confession of guilt and contrition. I think he feels it would offer a powerful stamp to the Church's warnings on secret societies."

"Couldn't you have fought them differently, da?"

Liam leaned to rest his arms across his knees and clasped his hands. The knocking of hammers outside and the drone of the nearby priest's voice reverberated off the stone walls.

"Which ever way was it that the workers hadn't already tried? Killing any man is a horrific thing, and a man trembles and prays his reasons are just when he orders it so."

Owen's eyes squeezed near shut; it was the closest Liam had come to telling him he'd ordered someone's killing.

Liam saw Owen's pain, and jabbed a finger into a palm, "Listen, Tecumseh Sherman said his boys were right in killing rebs, and Stonewall Jackson said his boys were right in killing Yankee invaders. The only just law while that terrible war was waged was what each general and his troops believed was just. Who was God with? The God-stricken Church blessed men on both sides. They couldn't both be right. But it was I who decided what side was just and whether my sons would go to fight for it. They believed in me and gave their lives for our cause. I had to decide in this fight, too, what was just. Was I then to back away from exacting a worker's justice because it needed taking the lives of tyrant mine owners?"

Owen started to speak, his voice choked, and he started again, "I don't know, da."

Liam nodded and lifted his hands in a resigned gesture. "One day the owners will have to answer for their own cruelty and greed in all this. Every worker's death in the mines, or of someone in his family from want, was in itself an assassination and a crime. The owners have tried to twist power into right and justice be damned. They only ever wanted our fear. More than a few Mollies convicted here and in Pottsville had not even a part in the assassinations. But it's all done with us now. The Mollies are finished."

They sat quietly, watching each other, fixing in memory this closing moment together. Liam asked about Aine, how she was.

"She's holding up," Owen said. "You'd be amazed, da—the statue is back in the window, the Infant of Prague." Liam's face lit up. He blinked a few times and cleared his throat. Owen asked, "Do you want me to try and get her up here?"

"No, no. I wouldn't want to put her through that," Liam said. "I don't want her last memories of me to be in this cage—and afterward."

They talked more, about work in the mines, and life in the mountains, as if Liam needed these shared memories to carry away with him. All the while they carefully avoided any mention of the noises outside. Each rap of a hammer stung somewhere behind Owen's eyes. If all the appeals and petitions failed, his da had to have enough courage to be brave to the end, without any knuckling under to the likes of Fr. Morrison. It wasn't much to hope for, but what else was left? Abruptly, the cell door opened and the jailer called for the visitors to leave. Owen and his da stood, said their good-byes and hugged, and Owen followed the priest out of the cell.

The weather had turned cooler by that September morning when Grover drove Owen and Maura with him to Roseburg. The sky was lit a dull, purple gray when they started out, and gradually brightened along a thin blue horizon as they got nearer the town. They drove straight to the livery, where Grover turned over his horses and wagon to a groom, and walked to the prison. Grover had a newspaper pass to enter as one of the official witnesses. He tried to talk the prison guard into letting Owen and Maura go in with him for a last visit with Liam. No entry without a written permit. Owen slumped against the stone archway. Grover put a hand on his shoulder and Maura stood close.

"I hoped I'd be able to watch da be brave to the end," Owen said. "They ought to have let me in." His voice was terrible, and he didn't know if he'd made any sense.

Grover looked down the street behind them. "If you really want to do it, there're some people gathering to watch from on top of that hotel. I know the owner; tell him I sent you and he'll let you up there."

Owen looked back. All along the street people were on balconies and rooftops with views overlooking the prison wall. "Will you go with me?" he asked Maura.

"I will," she said. "It may help if we both pray for his soul along the way."

"Prayer isn't going to change a thing. My da has to die today and we've both said the last prayers we'll ever say."

"Right—I was only saying." She was close to tears and kept pulling one hand through the other. "We'd better go now, there's getting to be a lot of people on that roof."

They left Grover and hurried down the street. The owner of the hotel had the outside stairway roped off, admitting only hotel guests and friends onto the roof. He let them by when they mentioned Grover, and they were barely in time to get a standing place along the front parapet wall. Soon the sun lifted higher and long dark shadows edged back from the center of the prison yard, gradually revealing the gallows platform. The ugly machine stood now in bare sunlight, and four looped ropes dangled from a crossbeam above the platform.

CHAPTER THIRTY-FOUR—The Last Walk

"My cousin said they had to use double four-by-twelve's for the crossbeam," a man alongside them said to his friend. "They're going to drop them four at a time and get it done with."

"Lord, God, won't that be something," his friend said, and he whistled. "I heard they'd never had a hanging in this county, yet. Hope they get this one right."

Owen folded his arms on the parapet wall and hung his head. Maybe it's a lucky mineworker that dies within just a few minutes of breathing Whitedamp. You go to sleep and just don't ever wake up. He thought a bit about what Maura had said, about prayers to help da make it through. But da already made his last confession, and no amount of prayers would change a thing.

A long time passed before there was any activity in the prison yard. Finally, as the morning chill lifted, Owen and Maura watched as people began entering the yard from inside the building. They searched for their nametags on chairs lined up in rows on the far side of the platform. Grover stood with a few men behind the last row of chairs.

A few minutes later the first of the prisoners was led out and a murmur went through the people on the roof. The prisoner was dressed in a black suit, a white shirt, and had a cluster of red flowers and a purple ribbon pinned at his lapel. He walked stiffly, accompanied on one side by a priest carrying a crucifix and on the other side by a prison guard. As that prisoner neared the platform a second, younger-looking prisoner was brought out. He, too, was dressed in a dark suit and had a cluster of yellow flowers and purple ribbon at his lapel. A priest carrying a crucifix accompanied him, too, and walking beside them, another guard. As the first man took his place on the gallows platform the priest handed him the crucifix, and the man kissed and clutched it as the priest made signs of a blessing. The second man knelt on both knees, holding to his crucifix as he was blessed. The awful procession continued, till four prisoners stood on the gallows platform. Owen's da was not among these.

The priests collected the crucifixes. One priest put a hand on the shoulder of a prisoner and gestured toward the rows of witnesses. Their faces at this distance were indistinct to Owen. The prisoner lifted his head and spoke to the witnesses. At times he received prompting by the priest to get through the pitiful ordeal. The other prisoners followed in like fashion, and when all were done, the priests stood at the side of the platform as the men were bound hand and foot with manacles, ropes were fitted over their necks, and white hoods were placed over their heads.

Owen couldn't decide whether he was going to watch, but a horrible fascination took hold, and he looked on as the trap doors were sprung.

The hoods of the men stayed visible just above the platform, and two of the men jerked and kicked for a few seconds after the drop. Owen laid his head on his arms and squeezed his eyes shut, taking long, rasping breaths. When he lifted his head again, the men had been taken down and were stretched out on the ground. The group of witnesses came forward by rows to view the still forms.

It wasn't long till the others were led out from the prison. The first fellow was without a jacket, just a white shirt and brown pants, and he walked with a spring in his step. He carried a bouquet of flowers wrapped in a ribbon and smelled them as he went. The next man was in a suit, and wore his flowers at his lapel like the others. He walked purposefully. Two of the same priests as before walked with the men. The third man out was Owen's da, and Fr. Morrison walked beside him. His da was without a jacket, just a billowing white shirt and sleeve garters, and he wore dark trousers. Some lavender flowers were tucked by their stems into one of his sleeve garters, and blue ribbon ends from the flowers whipped in the breeze as he walked. Owen took courage at seeing his da's strong gait, and he felt a respect for the first man's casual bravery, still smelling flowers as he'd mounted the stairs.

"I would never have expected those men to have worn the ribbons and flowers," Maura said. "It seems so unnatural for mine patch men."

Owen straightened up from leaning on the parapet and squeezed his eyes to better see the men on the platform. It was not until he felt a stinging sensation in his hands that he realized how hard he'd been rubbing the gritty surface of the parapet. He lifted a hand to see a raw bruising of his palm. "I think it's something taken from the early Mollies in Ireland, when they wore the sprigs and ribbons of a mythical hag on their sallies against the landlords."

Owen watched to see how the first man would act as his priest offered him the crucifix. The prisoner's nerve failed him; he turned away, clutching the bouquet to his chest, and hunched over, shaking. The second man became distraught and made an awful display of kissing his crucifix, and his priest tried to console him. He calmed down and clutched the crucifix to his chest. Owen's attention turned to da. Liam declined the crucifix Fr. Morrison offered him. He bowed his head, made the sign of the cross, and moved to take his position on a trap door.

"Aye, that and no more," Owen said, and sobbed before he could choke it off. Maura tightened her grip on his arm and people at his side turned to look at him. He squeezed the moist blindness from his eyes and strained to watch the ritual unfold to its dreadful end. When it came time for last words to the witnesses, the man with the flower bouquet laid it on the platform and stood silent with head bowed. The priest seemed to remonstrate with him a few minutes, then perhaps when he saw the man had reached some limit of his endurance, he blessed him and moved away. The second man handed back his crucifix and made a halting speech toward the witnesses, helped along by his priest. Owen shook his head.

And then it was Liam's turn. Fr. Morrison went to stand beside him and seemed to implore him to speak to the witnesses and reporters. Owen couldn't continue watching, his mind swirled and anguish tightened across his chest so that he could no longer breathe. He thought he might pass out and leaned on top of the parapet to keep his knees from buckling. He felt Maura grab and hold his arm. People around him talked excitedly, but Owen had lost any semblance of what was happening.

Maura thought to try leading him away from the parapet, but they were hemmed in by the frenzied crowd pressing in to see the approaching horror. She put an arm around Owen's shoulders to keep him from slipping back from the wall and forced herself to watch the final moments. The voices of the crowd rose toward a high pitch, suddenly interrupted by an eerie silence. A few whistles penetrated the silence, followed by a few coarse remarks, some callow cheers. and trailing off to murmurs and somber intonations. Maura's weeping began to be noticed and spectators standing nearby moved away from her and Owen. She kept an arm around his shoulders and used her other hand to grip the parapet, holding tight to keep him up on his feet.

Owen regained a gradual sense of where he was and felt a strength return to his legs. He whispered to Maura with her face next to his that he was over the dizziness now and he'd be all right. She eased back from him until she saw he could stand on his own.

"Where are we at with it?" Owen said, stepping tentatively back from the wall.

"It's done, Owen. They've carried Liam and the other men away." The tears still ran on her face and people leaving the rooftop gaped at them as they walked by.

Owen's tears came now, too. "Did he hold steady?"

"He did that."

"You're sure? No speech to the witnesses like Fr. Morrison wanted—sorry to the church and all the faithful for the troubles the Mollies brought?"

Maura sobbed a moment and choked through her words, "None of that, Owen. He said nothing."

CHAPTER THIRTY-FIVE—Farewell

Owen took a last look around the empty house. Eyes clouded over as memories flooded his mind, and he had to will his breathing back. Closing the door, he slung a canvas haversack over his shoulder, and stooped to pick up a small cloth satchel. Going up the pathway, he stopped and glanced across the echelons of hills. Everywhere trees turned color. Great swaths of red and gold marched up forested slopes. A few long, feathery clouds sailed over the twisting valley and a small bite of approaching cold lingered in the morning air. He'd miss all of it.

He left the path and entered onto the wagon trail toward town. A few women, doing laundry and hanging clothes in small yards outside their shanties, paused and watched him pass. A woman he knew called out a blessing and he called one back and a farewell with it. Others remained silent as he went by. The ghosts of the Mollies haunted people in different ways. Some lamented their passing, and others seemed relieved, anxious to have any of the Mollies' surviving kin gone too.

Later, on the train, he stared out at the hardwood forest flashing by. Da always seemed to know he couldn't win, but he'd been too fatalistic to turn aside. Fifteen Mollies hanged in that one terrible month and another five hanged afterward. Their story had become a sort of myth, fantastic things written about them in big city newspaper serials and in pulp magazines. In the end of it they'd been beaten, yes, but the labor violence didn't go away. It spread later from the mines to the railroad workers. Terrible newspaper stories kept coming out about workers killed in strikes and labor demonstrations kept the police busy all around the country. But for all of that, after the hangings the coal patches and the land of the Mollies had lain quiet.

The train conductor came through the car and Owen handed him a ticket. Hopmore to New York was a costly ride, but the railroad workers wouldn't see much of that money. Their wages were tight, too. Everyone was struggling to get by. Living on a mineworker's wages had only gotten harder, and the new union was too weak to help much. The railroad owners would not negotiate with the union, and wages in the mines had been cut further during the railroad workers' strikes. Revenues and profits had to come from somewhere, of course. Labor caused the shortfall; let it come out of their pay. Justice.

Owen took out Maura's letter and read it again. She'd gotten a job as a file clerk with a newspaper, didn't like the job, but held hopes of getting promoted into the advertising group to prepare copy. He set the letter aside and watched out the window. He'd been destroyed when Maura's family decided to call it quits and move to New York to live with relatives. She wrote him regularly while he'd continued working at The Anthracite Monitor. He spoke to Grover about leaving and Grover arranged an interview with a newspaper publisher in New York, a different paper than Maura's. Owen made a two-day trip there, and was offered a job as copy boy in the news section. Just a glorified messenger really, but it would be a foothold. During the time he'd returned home to clear his desk at Grover's paper, Aine went up to New York to find a place for them to live.

The train whistle blew again as his train eased away from the station, the last stop in the Northern Coal Field. A little way past the platform three tow-headed, ragamuffin boys stood in the scrub grass near the tracks and waved to the train. Probably getting close to ten years old, candidates for the breaker soon if they didn't stay in school. Owen waved back. He hadn't reached his goal of becoming a miner, but maybe he'd get to love this new career just as well. The old-time skilled miner was on short wages and tighter work rules now, and not much better off than common laborers.

Every class of worker was starving in the coal patch. Maybe he'd be writing one day about labor getting up off its knees, and remembering a debt to that ghost of the past, the Mollies, and the terrible, inescapable violence that led to a more just union labor in America.

www.ingramcontent.com/pod-product-compliance
Lightning Source LLC
Chambersburg PA
CBHW071136170626
46809CB00002B/647